I0633233

Clean,
A Tale of
The Inappropriate Library
by
Kim Isaac Greenblatt

Shockingly Awesome Press
Published In West Hills, California

Clean: A Tale of The Inappropriate Library
by Kim Isaac Greenblatt

Disclosure: The names, places and characters in this book are fictitious and any resemblance to anything living or dead is purely coincidental. This piece is a work of fiction. Libraries don't have books that can give you supernatural powers.

Or do they??? No, they don't. The real power you get is in knowledge.   In any case, support your local library and read a book, a comic book or watch an educational video. Failure in getting an education can contribute to the downfall of civilization. It also promotes ignorance. Ask questions and then listen to the answers! Then think if what you heard makes sense.

Published by Shockingly Awesome Press in West Hills, California, United States of America.

ISBN-13   978-0-9777282-9-9
Library of Congress Control Number: 2008902326

March 2008

Dedicated to Sharren, a great editor,
mother, wife and friend. Smoochies!

Just a reminder – The story in this book
takes place in the 1980s – there weren't any
cell phones back then and only primitive
Internet. It also takes place before the
events in "The Inappropriate Library."

TABLE OF CONTENTS

The Candy Man

September 4, 1989
Los Angeles, California 4:30 AM

The Candy Man didn't care what people would say. "Crack cocaine and crystal meth were here to stay," he would say to anybody who would listen to him.

But business really ate it this morning! He had to close up shop after being open a couple of minutes.

That didn't sit well with him.

Black Angus was having dry heaves as he staggered out of the visitor's lounge and started retching over a dresser. It was not the sound one hears from a big, black muscular bodyguard. It frightened the Candy Man.

He pushed his ammo clip into his Uzi (still the weapon of choice of drug dealers the world over) and nearly wet his worldly pants.

It would have been a great day, too.

His regular patrons were waiting quietly outside in the cold, silent pre-dawn dark lined up for their candy: the elderly Latino men with their pockmarked, leathery faces, the angry, tough talking street homeboys, the hookers – some of 'em real niiiice chicas.

The Candy Man, Rico Estavez, had been servicing the narcotic needs of the East Los Angeles community for many years. His crack house started out as a clearinghouse for migrants smuggled up north by the coyotes, the human flesh smugglers. Having managed to steer clear of local politics with the Bloods and Crips, the Candy Man got in on the drug trade before is was fashionable to just say "no".

He was also one of the few drug dealers who back in the day were successful at manufacturing crystal methamphetamine.

He'd laugh and say, "Ice and crack candy, bay-beee."

As far as Estavez was concerned, the war on drugs was over and his side won.

"Let Nancy Reagan or George Bush just try to take me out," he'd brag to his cholos.

The last thing he expected when his man, Jess, opened the reinforced, black painted steel doors at four-thirty in the morning to turn his $700 worth of ice into $30,000 cash was a big, shaggy bear mauling his customers.

At least he THOUGHT it was a bear.

"And why isn't that freakin' thing showing up on my cameras?" He asked nobody in particular.

It had carved poor Jess dead after Jess shot it.

Jess had pumped it full of bullets from his Uzi before it sped around the corner into an alley. Now Black Angus was sick. What was going on?

Black Angus turned his head up and gasped. His throat was swollen like somebody had stuffed it with sweat socks. He could barely breathe.

Rico Estavez ran into the stock room and slammed the door.

   The stock room was in the center of the modified four-bedroom crack house. It was reinforced with two feet of steel. A wall of Sony video monitors displayed the various rooms and exterior faces of the crack house. The cameras, being equipped for night vision, took in everything around the clock. He had spotted many a drug enforcement agent that way. Behind the Candy Man were boxes of supplies, food and ammunition.

   Estavez lifted the well-oiled trapdoor to the exit tunnel. He'd be damned if he would be caught like a rat like those other stupid dealers. No policeman, Nancy

Reagan or Geraldo Rivera would catch his butt.

A heck of a way to start a Monday.

And a freaking Labor Day, too! I should have taken the day off!

The Candy Man's fingers shivered against the cold steel of the trap door. The tunnel was dark. He snapped on a wall switch and a gasoline generator started humming. The lights below came on like several white eyes blinking open.

"All set, man. I can book on out of here anytime I want. And man, I mean anytime at all."

He turned towards the monitors. No bears. In fact, no nothing. All the screens had turned to snow. All of them except the one in the room that Black Angus was in. Angus had been with Estavez for a year now. Angus insisted on being called "Black Angus" because he thought of himself as an

unstoppable bull and because he was
proud that he was black.

When some of the junkies got too
whack-o, it was Black Angus who took care
of them. It was Black Angus who helped
Rico Estavez torture the Hawaiians that
tried to come in and take over his territory.
Angus was a righteous homeboy.

"And you are lettin' him die?" he asked
himself out loud.

Well, homeboy or not, business is
business.

"Check supplies, dude," he muttered to
himself.

Got the bullets. Got the band-aids.
Paper supplies all present and accounted
for: t.p., seat covers for those junkies who
had hepatitis and God Knows what else.

Mars bars. Water bottles.

He saw Black Angus lurch.

Estavez was glad that there weren't any microphones in the room. Fluids seemed to seep out of the dead man's body like he had sprung leaks.

From his mouth. From his fingers. From his nostrils. From the pores of his skin.

The liquid started crawling towards the room that Estavez was in.

"Not the time to lose it, bro, definitely not the time."

The Candy Man broke his cardinal rule about never mixing business with pleasure and grabbed a small pipe. He lit the ice and took a whiff. Bang!

The fluid moved closer to the door like a small wave lapping against the beach. The drug was starting to get to Estavez.

"Okay okay I'm getting paranoid and I am seeing things. Don't freak, don't you dare freak."

The steel doorjamb was starting to bend inward.

The doorjamb continued buckling inward on the door. A blue liquid seeped into the room like a spill. The solution began to pool by the door.

"Definitely no more drugs for me, homie."

The liquid fanned itself flat and began to bubble. The liquid solidified into a transparent blue claw.

The claw raised itself towards Estavez with five sharp-looking fingers.

Candy Man opened fire and the bullets sloshed through the appendage and smacked into the steel door. The slugs fell to the floor.

More fluid pumped itself into the room into the growing blue spot. The claw grew bigger.

Estavez dove into the tunnel. His heart was slamming in his chest and he was sorry he did the ice. He stumbled down the steps and yanked the spring lever that crashed the escape hatch behind him with a "boiiing" sound.

"Am I going nuts? What kind of claw was that?"

He sprinted down the tunnel. It was lit by sixty-watt bulbs every twenty feet. One hundred yards to go.

Just one hundred yards to go to the door to the streets. Time to shut down all rational thought for a while.

"Man, just hotwire a car and book on outta this neighborhood and chill for awhile."

Just run for it now, bad boy.

Something wasn't right here and just thinking about it too much was only going to make things worse.

Seventy-five yards to go.
"Gotta be some crap the Bloods are trying to pull on me. Some special effects crap from the studio like that video, "FX", I rented. Or that T2 movie – yeahhhh, buddy."

Man, you can do anything with special effects these days.

Fifty yards to go.

The lights flickered.

Something had gotten to the generator. That fluid that was blue. Like ice.

Ice, man. "Should have called myself 'Iceman' that sounds cooler."

Kick it, Estavez. Twenty-five yards.

Ten yards.

The hall reeked of alcohol.

Five yards.

He could see the door open to the back alley that would lead him to freedom. He could smell the taco man cart's food cooking!

"Out the door, up a few steps and everything's going to be bueno."

Then he was gonna nail the freakers that were messin' with him.

The thought suddenly struck him that the door was open.

"Where did that freakin' bear run off to?"

Something very big threw itself on his chest, catapulting him into a wall.

The Candy Man had his answer.

Tenderfoot

September 4, 1989
Northwest Star Scout Camp 3:00 AM

Ninety minutes before Rico Estavez was murdered, Patrick Brighton bolted upright in his Holofil sleeping bag. Something was scrunching the brown leaves outside his blackened Baker tent. He looked at his watch. The luminous hands of his chronometer displayed three zero zero.

He thought he was listening to the sounds of the older, Second Class, First Class and Eagle Scouts as they were positioning themselves for some new form of outdoor ambush for the eleven year-old Tenderfoot.

Being initiated into Troop 240 sucked.

When Nick Saffold told him earlier things like, "The other guys left me tied naked to a Joshua tree and left me there overnight," Patrick got more and more terrified.

The more he thought about it, the more ridiculous it seemed.

"What's to be scared of?" he asked himself.

This morning, there were plenty of things to scare him.

Patrick rubbed his eyes with his fists and started telling himself that this would pass.

"Just ride it out, Mr. Brighton, and you will be a full-fledged Boy Scout."

But he didn't buy it.

He wasn't getting much sleep this campout anyways since his tent was on an incline next to a stream.

Instead of lulling Patrick to sleep with its continual cascading on the stones, the water kept him up most of the last three nights. He was the last boy to be initiated on this trip.

He managed the pantsing the night before with a grin-and-bear-it attitude. The jog back naked from the outhouses was only one hundred yards. At least they left him his shoes.

Something about this morning's initiation didn't feel right.

The scrunching, paper like sound stopped and a shuffling started coming from outside the tent by Dan Hunsinger. But it wasn't the giggling, guffawing sound that jerkwads make when they are about to lash a bowline around your sleeping bag to tie you up with.

It was an animal sound.

It even smelled animal.

Patrick quietly unzipped this sleeping bag. He peered into the darkness, saw nothing and fingered around for his flashlight. He held his breath.

A moaning sound upset the cadence of the stream.

He exhaled and strained his hearing.

Moaning. Then a quiet, subtle clawing against a tree.

The tent was darker than the inside of a dirty boot.

The Baker was open by Patrick and Dan's feet. There was no floor to the tent. The scout campgrounds were especially black tonight since there was no moon and the clouds effectively shut out the stars.

There were no flaps for the tent by the boys' feet. They were the new scouts so they didn't get their dibs on the tents with the floors. Their bedding was simple, consisting of a plastic ground cloth and their sleeping bags. There were no campfires since it was very early in the morning. There was no glow from night skylights since they were miles away from the nearest city.

Patrick whispered, "Danny."

Danny rolled away from him.

"Danny, wake up. There is something outside our tent."

Nothing.

Danny slept like the dead. He heard nothing.

"I think we've got a mountain lion outside the tent or the guys are playing with us."

A twig snapped.

Like something leaning too hard and tearing a tent's mosquito netting.

It moved closer.

"Danny, get up."

Danny was out of it. Between his initiation and the day's Camporee activities he could sleep through an earthquake. In fact, his mother said that he did once.

Patrick thought about turning on his light outside the tent. Maybe the boys or potential cougar could be spooked. But the cats never came down this far on the hills.

"This scout (or cat) knows that I am on to it."

Patrick aimed the flashlight through the opening of the tent by his feet. He nervously drummed his finger on the sliding switch of the Eveready light.

If it were the boys, he'd have the element of surprise on his side for a change. He took the precaution of going to bed fully dressed the night before.

And his flashlight was one of the expensive Halogen ones that could blind them, too!

The moaning sound approached the foot of his sleeping bag in the darkness.

Something yanked on his sleeping bag.

Patrick snapped the flashlight on and piercing, white beam illuminated the night. He winced at the sudden loss of his night sight.

The beam illuminated the camping area. The silhouettes of other tents were displayed further down the slope but there was nothing creepy or cougar outside the Baker tent.

Danny groaned in his sleep. He covered his head with the folds of his sleeping bag and sank into the bag like a caterpillar into a cocoon.

Patrick didn't hear or smell the thing anymore. He knew though that the other scouts were masters of psychological torture that would rival the CIA and KGB and he should face his fears. Patrick rolled open his unzipped sleeping bag, snaked towards his feet and leaned very slowly out the back of the tent, listening.

Just the stream.

Mom was right (as usual). One's fears vanish when confronted. Patrick shined the light around the outside of the tent and slowly rose to his feet. He inspected the tent and its lashings. The wooden poles were in place. The stakes and lines were securely fastened. He paused to relax the tension from his shoulders.

Something scampered from behind him.

Patrick whirled and aimed his light in the direction of the sound. It was from the Silver Pine tree. The reddish tree had grown at an angle along the slope and its branches were covered with ling, slender purple cones. The light failed to disclose anything remotely out of place.

"Could the cat or scout have climbed the tree?" he asked himself. "The limbs don't look strong enough on the tree to support anything."

He shined his light upwards through the cones. The campground was chosen for its beauty and for its trees. It was one of the few sites where one didn't have to worry about the fire line and starting a forest fire. The cones converged into a dark mass and Patrick couldn't make out a thing.

Behind him, something splashed in the stream.

Patrick whirled and thought he caught a glimpse of something.

Whatever it was, it wasn't in the beam of his flashlight. Patrick was tense again. He wasn't a momma's boy, but he wished she were with him right now.

"Mom always had all that rational, make sense stuff for everything."

Whenever Patrick use to get spooked, she always would say something smart to get Patrick to not be afraid.

But that is what initiations were about. To send you on stupid hunting trips for imaginary animals called snipes.

To get you afraid. To embarrass you.

"I wish I decided to skip scouting."

What would a super hero do in a situation like this? Well, probably use some super radar or hearing and zoom in on the bad guy and blast 'em or beat him up. Patrick didn't have any weapons or super powers but the fact he was trying to act on his fear made him feel a little better.

He quickly moved closer to the stream.

Nothing but the sound of running water.

Patrick shined the light up and down the length of the stream and watched the light bend as it went beneath the surface at some points and reflected on the stones.

Something took a swipe at his leg.

Patrick yelped and whirled.

There was nothing there but something had scratched at his pants leg. There was a stinky smell there as well. He shined the light around looking for the culprit.

Nothing.

There were some mumblings from some of the other tents. His yelp had been louder than he thought.

"Hey, you played with yourself too hard there, buddy."

"Awright, knock it off, you guys."

A cry came back from a tent, "Shuddup. We've got a long drive back in the morning."

Patrick looked at the pants leg.

He sniffed it.

It was an animal smell but he couldn't place it. It sure wasn't a cat smell. He smelled wet dogs before and it wasn't a dog.

He cautiously made it back to the tent. If he continued to cry out now, he'd be called a wuss.

He investigated the foot of his sleeping bag. There was a slight tear in the bag. But there was no scent. He examined it closer.

"Whatever had made the rip couldn't have been anything too big," he tried to tell himself.

He looked at his jeans. He rolled his pants leg up. Thankfully, his skin wasn't broken and he wasn't cut. His pants though were stinky.

"What is this? What would a super hero detective do? Or even mom?"

The answer to both questions would be to analyze what happened. Mom was a doctor of forensics and could handle all the unusual and gross stuff pretty well.

"What we have here, Mr. Brighton is some average-sized (please don't be big), unknown creature that has a stink about it."

Why wasn't the stink on the sleeping bag?

"First I gotta isolate the smell. It isn't skunk. Not cat or dog."

Patrick leaned forward and sniffed again. He heard other people mucking about in their tents. With the noise of the other scouts, Patrick felt assured that this critter wouldn't be coming back.

"My God. What if it was something small and with teeth like in the movie,

'Critters'? What if it was an outlaw alien that ate people? Aw, think stupid."

"If it were an outlaw alien, it wouldn't have settled for just taking a swipe at you."

Patrick bent over and shimmied back into his tent. He was starting to feel pretty hot from his running around and from being under his sleeping bag with his clothes on. He unzipped his pants and pulled them down his legs. It smelled of something he had smelled before.

He placed the pants by his face and took a whiff.

"Smell reminds me of Mom."

It reminded him also of school.

The lab.

Something funky alright...

Form-al-da.. the cleaning crap that was used in frogs in biology as a preservative.

Formaldehyde.

Like the stuff Mom used on some of the stiffs. The pants smelled like formaldehyde and some kind of animal.

But definitely formaldehyde.

What kind of animal smelled of formaldehyde? It was used to preserve dead things. And what was it doing on his pants and not his sleeping bag?

"There's a rational explanation for all of this. I'm sure as soon as I figure out what it is I'll feel like a real dweeb for feeling so scared."

It had to be some kid.

It just had to be.

There was a scratching outside the tent.

Patrick turned and leaned outside the tent with his flashlight aimed at the tree. Something had climbed the tree.

Something big.

Something fast.

Something that growled.

Try as he might, Patrick couldn't get his light clearly on the thing. It scampered higher into the treetop and the light seemed to go through it.

"Fine by me", he said. Patrick reclined on the top of his sleeping bag and clicked off the light.

"What the heck is that thing? A big ferret? Ha!"

It would be daylight soon and Patrick could play detective further once they struck camp. All the excitement started to finally get to Patrick and he started to close his eyes.

In that borderline state between consciousness and sleep, Patrick realized that the animal had placed his (hers? its?) scent on him.

Like a dog or lion staking territory.

But most dogs and lions don't usually make moans and move around quietly.

And this creature didn't want physical territory, like Patrick's sleeping bag.

Or even Patrick's pants.

It wanted Patrick.

Good Morning

September 4, 1989
Los Angeles Coroner's Office 6:30 AM

The two most important things in Dr. Jan Brighton's life right now were that her son get back safely from his first scouting trip and that she finish her black coffee without any interruptions Ron Adamovich stuck his head in the door to her office, "Good morning, Dr. Brighton. Did you sleep well?"

She sighed. So much for important item number two. "Whenever you get formal, Ron, I know it's been a busy night. Whatcha got?"

"You can finish your coffee first, if you like."

"God, Ron, It must be really grisly. Come clean."

"There's been a series of murders in East Los Angeles. They are pretty grisly."

"How many?"

"Six."

"Six? Gang related?"

"Too soon to tell. It's at a shooting gallery and crack house that we've been eyeballin' and were ready to move on. Rumor had it that the owner had a crystal meth lab, too."

"I think I will finish my coffee first."

Ron smiled. She liked it when Ron smiled. He was so hard working all the time. He looked like a heavy-set old school actor from the 1940's or 1950's. Homicide was a hard place for a detective. The hours were long. Ron still managed to smile and look good doing it too.

She took a gulp of coffee and replaced the half-full mug that read, "YOU NAB 'EM, WE SLAB 'EM" on her desk. Jan stood up. This would be a real bad time for her because her assistants were swamped or on vacation. "So what's with the six?"

Ron's smile disappeared. "You'll have to see for yourself. It's like something that happened back with the Poker killings."

She remembered all too well the so-called Poker killings and the all too graphic violence of severed baby heads and mutilated corpses. Each corpse was left with five cards representing a poker hand. The killer eventually got sloppy and was identified by some of his own prints that were found on one of the victims. That nightmare lasted for three months.

She forced the thoughts from her head. "I suppose I should be grateful that you didn't wake me up at two in the morning." Though it really wouldn't have mattered if he had called. She didn't sleep much the last three days because she was worried about Patrick.

"We didn't get the call until about an hour or so ago. Of course, next time I can call you at two in the morning and chat with you sometimes, if you'd like."

"Huh."

"Is that a 'yes huh' or a 'no huh'?"

"Just a 'huh-huh'. I was thinking about Patrick."

*

"Oh he'll be fine." Ron was the one who talked Jan and Patrick into considering scouts. Judging from Jan's worried expression and the fact that she was getting to work incredibly early for the last few days he was wondering if it had been a mistake.

Ron use to have the time of his life in scouts and was hoping Patrick would have the same. But boys could be pretty crappy to one another.

Jan tried to force a smile. "It's just that as a mother, I worry, you know?"

Ron admired her small, thin figure. Her black hair was starting to turn gray and Ron thought that made her more attractive. For being a single, working mother in her late thirties, Dr. Brighton was quite a success story. That scared Ron sometimes.

"I get it," he said. "Thanks for not adding 'Wait until you are a mother'."

"Ahh, you already are a mother, Ron."

They both laughed.

Why do I even open my mouth some days, Ron asked himself. I shouldn't have brought up scouts. She probably hates me for mentioning it.

"Listen, if scouting doesn't work out for Patrick, I promise to take him camping myself, okay?"

*

"That sounds fine but that is also a conversation we need to table for another time." He tries so hard to be nice, Jan thought.

So why do I treat him so rotten, like now?

Because he's a man like my ex-husband, Gilberto Garcia, and I am feeling pretty angry now.

She remembered Gilberto enough to remind herself that she dumped that selfish bastard as well as his name. She legally changed her name and Patrick's back to her maiden name. She forced the rising angry thoughts from her head.

"We've gotta get going on these homicides, Ron. Let's rock."

Ron opened and held the door for her. They left her office.

It was a lousy morning for a lousy day.

*

Outside of Jan's office was a small closet for the janitor. The door was locked. Inside the closet was a silver bucket with a wringer and a mop. There was some murky, black water inside the bucket left over from the cleaning man from the night before. A blue stream of water had shot out of the bucket and shaped itself into a human ear. After a few seconds of trying to track Jan, the blue water returned into the blackish water and bubbled.

Preparations

The coroner's van started to slow down. Jan Brighton started running through her preparations in her head. It gave her something to do and kept her sharp. Rustled up some deputy examiners. They are on their way. Check.

"Did you radio ahead to the officers at the scene? Check. Med kit in van? Check."

She noted the sky. It was smoggy.

No wonder her eyes burned.

Forget your eyes. Keep your head clear and stay on the routine. Without a routine, you make mistakes.

"Bag in the van? I went over that. Check. Lab gear, check. Camera, check." She glanced at the clock on her dash and it was about two minutes to seven.

The houses they drove past were a patchwork quilt of well-kept California Mission homes with splendid front-lawns or gardens and abandoned ghost bungalows. The one common denominator to all the houses was the bars on their windows. Jan felt uncomfortable.

It was more than the smog. The reason Jan felt uncomfortable was because East Los Angeles had worked hard at making the neighborhood drug free. She was riled because the filth of crime soiled the Latino community that lived, worked and played in East L.A.

Not that Latinos all of a sudden had a monopoly on crime. People get raped, robbed and murdered all over. It just hit her harder because it reminded her that Patrick still had to grow up in a city that sometimes wasn't very forgiving or safe.

"Enough of those delightful thoughts", she said to herself.

"Huh, done talking to yourself yet?"
Ron asked. He sneezed almost as if on cue.

She smiled. "Bless you." The smog got
to him, too. Had to be a Stage Three alert.
Traffic hasn't even picked up yet this
morning and we are already dying from the
air.

Poor Ron. He often told her that moving
to L.A. from Miami was one of the worse
things that he did. Ron would get on his
medical examiner jag and confide that
riding shotgun in the van made him antsy.
Even though he had come to terms with
death on the job working Vice and
especially in Homicide, the van still
represented the cold, final trip of the Last
Ride. They didn't talk about it often.

"It was better than riding in the back,"
she'd often say.

The van reached City Terrace and Alma.
She parked between two squad cars. One
patrolman was replacing a yellow saw horse
to keep out the looky-loos while another

officer strung out several more yards of yellow police barricade streamers.

We're having a bright, happy Labor Day block party, she thought to herself.

Jan got out of the van and slammed the door. She was carrying her lab gear. Ron had practically jumped out of the van before it had stopped and was already talking to a detective. Ron's hair had that tousled look. His strong arms tightened against his white, long sleeved shirt. She wondered if he could pass as a model for some corporate executive for a Sear's catalog.

Back to business, chica.

Jan had studied Spanish in college and that was an added plus to her day-to-day dealings in Los Angeles. Her ex was Mexican. Jan use to impress him with her command of the language.

She turned to the detective that Ron was talking to. The crowds of local thrill seekers moved closer to the barricades. A man was being escorted into a car by a police officer and for a very brief moment, Jan felt a tingling up and down her spine. She tried to get a closer look at the man but the police car took off and the crowd of people closed ranks in front of her like a zipper.

Dink Cruthers, a balding detective from the Columbo Detective School of fashion, was wearing his crumpled, tan raincoat. The man wiped his brow with his sleeve. It was already eighty degrees. It was going to be a miserable day outdoors. They were standing in front of a dark, almond brown California Mission house sandwiched between two project buildings. There was a black door half open to the building. The detective looked like he had been inside and he had been sick.

It was gonna be a big one, she thought.

"What's up? How are we doing?" Jan asked.

Dink shrugged his shoulders. "As best as can be. We've cold-shouldered a live-action team from KTLA already and the word has gotten out that we want no press for awhile."

Dink's facial features tightened. This meant that it was a real big and bad one. We wouldn't want any copycat killings from people reading the papers, listening to the radio or watching TV.

They started walking to the house.

"How many now?" Ron asked.

"Still six. Three locals and three gunslinger Jesse James types. They were a local junkie, a hooker, a snitch and from the prelims the three guys who worked this fine establishment."

Jan sniffed. It had a smell. That dead smell. Something else, too. Cleaning smells.

Two uniformed policemen were standing next to several covered body parts off to the left of the front door. Somebody or some bodies were apparently cut into pieces. There was blood on the front door. A broken video camera was lying on the grass with its wires to the house still intact and strung out like black and red spaghetti. The body parts and blood reminded Jan of meatballs in a hearty meat sauce. I should share that with Ron.

Better get busy and forget the M.E.'s sense of humor.

"Ron and I will take it from here. I'm expecting some back up and I want to get this done as quickly as possible. If this thing has to be kept quiet, I want things wrapped up and back at my lab ASAP."

"Got it." Dink's baldhead was shining with perspiration.

"If you don't mind some free medical advice, why don't you take off your coat and grab something cool to drink?"

Dink had a jack-o-lantern smile from having a few of his front teeth missing. "I'm not thirsty and I can't. My coat is like my shield, you know?" He was sweating thick droplets of perspiration, which made Jan want to throw him a sponge.

"You know I always wear my coat. Day or night, hot or cold. It's my lucky charm and I figure as long as I wear it, everything will be all right. It's like my bulletproof vest, you know? Sort of keeps me from thinking about ending up like one of those poor souls."

Dink pointed to one of the bags.

Jan could see that he was getting over-heated.

"Come on, Dink, I'll go over your head if I have to so please take five minutes and go get yourself something to drink. You're going to get dehydrated and get sick if you aren't careful."

"Yeah, I hear you, so just get on with it, okay?"

She knew he probably wouldn't listen to her. He was from the old ball busting, Mean Macho Machine Superbull School of stubborn men. Her ex-husband was like that. In some ways, she could understand that kind of thinking. His coat was his lucky rabbit's foot and it worked for him.

Like her going over lists in the van on the way to crime scenes. She could understand why he wouldn't want to take it off around here, too.

Have I blown it? Is he going to hamper my investigation?

"I probably shouldn't have said anything", she thought to herself silently. "Probably threatened his masculinity which was the last thing that I wanted to do to anybody."

When her husband deserted her and Patrick, she was struggling through medical school and at the time she was feeling terrible that she had not been a good wife to him.

Having him walk out like that was the best thing that could have happened to her. Her career had taken off and Patrick was doing okay without a dad.

Or was he?

Jan knew that she could be over-protective. She sometimes wished she had someone she could compare notes with. No time for that with two full time jobs as a mother and as a medical examiner. So she better get back to the latter or she'll not be able to afford the former!

Dink started unbuttoning his coat. He removed it and placed it in one of the detective's cars.

"Good for him," she thought, "But I will never say another word again to him in front of other cops."

Jan took another deep breath (a big mistake from the smell of it) and bent over the first victim. She took out a surgical mask and put it on.

She lifted up the blanket.

It was the bottom half of a woman and it was covered with blood and the contents from its emptied intestines.

"Dink, I'm sorry. Can you let me wear your raincoat for a while? I could use some good luck now..."

Peanuts

Jan's Lab 9:00 AM

"What did you find?"

"Peanuts."

"Peanuts?"

"I just finished doing the hooker's stomach in the section of the torso that was found severed from the body. I found partially digested peanuts in her stomach."

Ron smiled. "Salted or un?"

"Un", Jan started pulling off her bloodstained surgical gloves. She had been at her work since they made it back to the station. The operating tables were something out of an abattoir. Both Ron and Jan moved towards the exit. Jan picked up her clipboard. She was very neat about her notes. She worked very hard at keeping her paperwork clean and nearly stain-free. A ceiling microphone cable connected to a tape recorder in her office was dangling like a snake from a tree.

She sometimes would take verbal notes, while working but the mike was currently dead. Like her clients...

"What else?"

"By the book?"

"For starters?"

They entered Jan's adjoining office and closed the door. She noted Ron's brow relax. He definitely should be a male model. Jan thumbed through her notes.

"For starters, the young missy had a busy night. There were three types of semen found in her vagina. Two types in her stomach."

"I guess she didn't worry about AIDS".

"Most junkies don't. The deceased had a severed torso, several abrasions on all pieces of the body found, subcutaneous hemorrhaging throughout the system and her pieces were in full rigor. She had substantial blood loss and lividity consistent with the findings. Blood tests show evidence of heroin abuse and she was slightly anemic."

Ron tensed up again. "She was messed up really bad. What's your guess as to what did it to her, Doctor? A PCP case?"

"No, a trained animal."

Ron paused. "So you think what the witness said might be true?"

"Yeah, there were no fingerprints on any of the bodies. Even an angel duster would leave prints."

"This is bad. Anything to go on?"

"God knows. The most bizarre thing is there were no tracks. Wait, scratch that. The most bizarre, bizarre thing is that two of the bodies, the dealers inside the house, were really strange. One shows death by asphyxiation and the other was literally smashed into pieces against that wall in the tunnel. Both were reeking of alcohol, water and ammonia."

"That cleaning sort of smell."

Jan nodded. "I can't figure out why somebody's killing with a trained animal and then using window cleaner on the victims, too. It sure wasn't a satanic ritual I've heard of."

Ron smiled. "If it weren't so serious it would be funny. It reminds me of that Steve Martin film, you know, the 'Man with Two Brains' or something. Merv Griffin played the window cleaning fluid killer in it. That is some pretty sick stuff."

"Got that right." She skimmed her notes. "Okay, what did I miss? No clean prints. I've also got too many other cases to worry about. Think."

What kind, if any, cult? What's with the animal angle? Her assistants were busy in the next room running their tests.

She went into the next room. Myra Lewis, an attractive assistant in her twenties was writing notes as she peered into a microscope.

"Anything new, Myra?"

The younger woman turned her head away from the microscope and tossed her long, blonde hair back. "No, if I look at this tissue sample any longer I think I will die."

"Do the best you can."

Jan went back into her office with Ron. No sense in bothering any other of the assistants until they come forward with something. Jan looked at Ron. "Your turn."

"That one witness was the only person who seems willing to talk, if in fact, there were any other witnesses left alive."

"His name?"

"His street name is 'Injun Joe.' You probably saw him as we got to the scene. He was being escorted back to the station under our protection."

That was the man who made Jan feel funny. "A real Native American? Or is he from Central or South America?" Los Angeles was home to a large population of people lumped in as Indians.

"Who knows, he was the one who made the call to report the murders. He was trying to score a drink."

"Great, so the only witness we have is a possible alcoholic. At least we've got something to work with. What was he doing associated with the likes of those dealers?"

"They liked him. He ran errands for them in exchange for booze money. This guy came running back from a gofer run for something and he found our dead hooker, a

Miss Angeline Blush. He went around, saw the carnage, got spooked and called us from a pay phone at the liquor store. The prints came in on the other victims. Interested?"

"Very. Who are they?"

"The dead locals in the front of the house were Paolo Hernandez and Mark Jones, a couple of junkies. Jones dealt a little on the side to pay for his habit. The dead dealer with the gun was Jess Robbins. The black man was Angus Reeves and the man in the tunnel was Rico Estavez, aka 'The Candy Man'."

Jan smiled. "Who can take a rainbow, wrap it in with drugs?"

Ron laughed, "This Candy Man can't. He might have but he can't now."

"Criminal records?"

"Big ones. Reeves, Robbins and Estavez were into the scene heavily. We found their ice lab, too. There were a lot of local ladies who were selling themselves to get a smoke of crystal meth."

Jan thought about the kind of men who encouraged or forced women to become prostitutes to pay for their drug habits. Some girls were selling themselves for as low as two dollars in Los Angeles to support their habits.

"This Indian, uh, Injun Joe, what do you make of him?"

"See for yourself. When do you want to talk to him?"

"Now okay?"

"Sure."

She turned to a fresh page in her notebook. She assumed the detectives already had a tape recorder in the room with the witness but she also trusted her own notes. If the witness was too antsy, she could cool it on the notes and let the tape recorder pick up the conversation.

Jan tried to get her mind off of Angeline Blush. To live a life of drugs, hooking and poverty was bad enough. To die horribly by being ripped apart was even worse.

She turned towards Ron.

He's got strong looking jaws, she thought. I wonder what it would be like to go camping with him and Patrick one day.

Back to business, Dr. Brighton.

*

In the supply closet, a pair of blue liquid ears hovered on the surface like two small radar dishes. The ears were pointing towards Jan and Ron.

They listened.

The Rambler

Mr. Pym drove the aqua colored station wagon through the dense forest at fifty miles per hour. Patrick was in the back seat and looking over the scoutmaster's shoulder. Half a tank of gas.

Hope we don't get stranded.

He sat back and rubbed his black hair with his hand. Boy, does it need a wash. He turned towards Danny. Patrick was the same height and weight as Danny Hunsinger, his tent mate, but Danny's strawberry blonde hair never seemed to look dirty.

The caravan of scout cars broke up about twelve miles back as the other scoutmasters and parents took different routes to the freeway. Danny and Patrick were lucky to ride back to Los Angeles with Mr. Pym.

*

Mr. Pym was happy. He liked taking the scenic route back to town. He checked briefly on his charges in the rear view mirror and caught a glimpse of himself. His tanned, healthy features made him look younger than he was.

Not bad for a forty-two year old math teacher.

His own son was too young to go camping yet and it helped him forget the drudge of teaching fractions and algebra to kids who didn't seem to care. It brought back memories of when he was a Boy Scout.

*

Patrick turned towards Danny and caught a glimpse of Mr. Pym. The man's eyes returned to the road in front of him. Danny was in the front seat next to Mr. Pym. He was leaning against the window on the passenger side. His face was pressed against the glass, asleep.

Typical.

Patrick stretched his arms over his head and became aware of the tires rolling on the road. The continual rolling of the wheels on the gravel, the tar and leaves helped Patrick with his thinking. As tired as he was, the sounds kept him awake.

A quick inspection of the camping area in the morning revealed nothing to Patrick about the creature that sprayed him. None of the other scouts reported anything different after he hinted about seeing the thing last night.

They didn't tease him TOO badly.

The stupid wieners.

"Quick better call Batman, homeboy".

"Monsteros aqui? Aiee!"

"Hey, the little puss got scared, spooky-spooky."

The problem with understanding English and Spanish is that you can get treated like crap in both languages!

Patrick bent over and sniffed his pants. The scent seemed to have worn off but he couldn't shake the feeling that he was marked. It was like the feeling he use to get when his late Great Aunt Martha use to kiss him. After he'd wipe off her purple lipstick (yuchh! Auntie Bozo the Clown) he could still feel the phantom pressure of her lips on his cheek for an hour afterwards.

Patrick turned and inspected the backpacks as well as the rest of the gear in the back of the wagon.

All secure.

His gear had that slightly mildew scent from sleeping in the Baker tent. He thought about digging out a comic book. Hmmm. They were forbidden on Mr. Pym's camping trips. He decided to leave the book in his pack. Mr. Pym liked Patrick and he didn't want Pym mad at him.

"I gotta start working out more," he thought to himself. He got called "skinny" by the other boys. Both he and Danny were ragged on by the bigger boys because the scouts knew they could get away with it. For now, at least.

Patrick yawned and caught himself staring out the window. The trees rolled past him like those fake backgrounds that kept looping at the Universal Studios Tour in those cheap-o gangster films. Like where the car is always driving by the same stretch of stupid road. He loved the new Star Trek show and remembered the giant phone that he and his Mom played on a few years ago.

Something caught his eyes in the woods.

Something BIG was running through the woods pacing his car. Something that could keep up at FIFTY MILES PER HOUR.

It's a three-wheeler. No, too big.

His heart started beating faster.

Awright, it's an off-road four-by-four.

No, wrong shape.

The large brown beast turned its head while it was running. Patrick started trembling as he saw two quick flashes of the whites of his eyes.

It was a bear.

No, not just a bear. It was THE bear. Patrick knew instinctively that this was the thing that was after him at the campsite.

"What am I going to do?"

If I say anything to Mr. Pym, he'll think I'm nuts. He'll say stuff about me reading too many comic books and watching too many horror movies.

Worse, Danny will laugh at me and tell the other guys.

The bear was deep enough in the woods
to not be clearly seen anymore. But Patrick
knew that the beast smelled him. Just as
somehow, Patrick knew it was the same
creature that marked him early this
morning.

A bond had been formed between the
two of them and Patrick was keenly aware
of the discomfort he was feeling. It wasn't
the kind of bond between buddies: a palsy-
walsy, howzitgoin' dude kind of friendship.

It was the kind of relationship between
predator and prey.

*

The wagon slowed down. It was a good,
used car. The Rambler was well preserved
because Californians didn't usually have
the rust, salt, snow or spray to worry about
that car owners in other parts of the
country had. Smog wasn't a problem either
because Mr. Pym use to get his car washed
(water shortages or not) every week at some

different church's fund-raising car wash each week.

Mr. Pym had been taking care of the car for years. It was a good, workhorse of a car. By keeping it in good condition he supported local churches and kept his memories of his father taking him camping in it alive.

Up ahead, the road dropped into a series of blind hills. Playing it safe, Mr. Pym started slowing the Rambler down.

*

The bear-thing slowed.

Patrick was afraid that he was going to scream like a little girl. He summoned all of his strength and tried not to make his voice sound like Mickey Mouse.

"Danny".

Danny opened his eyes. "Huh?"

"Danny, what's that out your window in the woods?"

Mr. Pym glanced out Danny's window as the car started descending a hill.

Trees.

"Didn't see anything, Patrick. What was it?"

"I don't know, a deer, maybe."

Danny looked out the window. "Some campout, huh?"

"Yeah."

Mr. Pym checked his rear view mirror and side mirror.

"Have a good time, gentlemen?"

"Okay, I guess." Patrick kept straining to see what was outside the window. The bear was playing hide and seek.

Mr. Pym turned back to the approaching hill. Patrick could feel the change in the road as they started to climb. He wished that he hadn't eaten that cold Hungry Man Chile for breakfast. The two-lane highway ahead was empty.

Nothing but trees on either side of them.

"They get better, guys. The first one with the initiations is the worst. But cheer up. On the next campout, you guys can help give the initiations."

Patrick doubted that.

He saw the bear creature again.

Except this time it was farther along in the woods.

Ahead of the Rambler.

"How fast can deer or bears run, Mr. Pym?"

"Pretty fast. You think you saw a bear, Patrick?"

"Uh, yeah."

Danny chimed in. "I don't think they can run as fast as a car. If it were a cheetah, manohman, those cats can go up to seventy per!"

"Can bears run that fast?"

Mr. Pym was pausing for a long time. That told Patrick that he was thinking or he didn't really know.

"Don't think so. Even if a bear could, I don't see how through a forest as thick as this he could hit even ten miles per hour."

The Rambler had gone up and over the hill. The car was rising up another hill.

Patrick continued peering out his window. "Ah."

Danny Hunsinger rolled down his window with several quick squeaks of the window crank.

"Pee-ewe"

Mr. Pym made a face. "Roll it up, please. Something smells like somebody disinfected the entire forest or something."

It was the scent of formaldehyde.

Hunsinger couldn't crank it up fast enough.

Mr. Pym's window was rolled down and he cranked it up just as fast. The smell had wafted in from his side of the window, too.

"The wind'll blow in some strange stuff, guys."

Patrick bit his left knuckle.

It wanted him. It was following him. The bear was playing with him. Cat and mouse. Patrick had watched a neighbor's cat bring home a live mouse once and was mesmerized as the cat would nibble and claw at the tiny beast, push it away and watch it try and make a break. The cat would then recapture it. He thought it was pretty rad at the time but now it upset him. He silently muttered a prayer to God and sank his teeth into his hand.

Danny turned around. "Y'okay?"

"Yeah, I, um, just hurt my knuckle."

He took it from his mouth and could see the teeth marks indented in his skin.

"I just wanted to say thanks for bunking with me, Pat."

"No prob, Danny, anytime, bud."

"Good, homes. Us tenderloins gotta stay tight."

They both smiled at the nickname they were called over the long weekend.

BAM!

The Rambler had just come over the next hill when something big and fast rammed into the passenger front side of the wagon. With a lurch, the car was forced into a fishtail spin over to the other side of the road. Mr. Pym managed to pump the brakes till the car stopped moving.

Whatever had hit the car was gone.

Patrick watched Mr. Pym slip the car into "P" for park. His heart was racing. Mr. Pym turned around and faced the boys, a look of genuine concern on his face.

"You guys okay?"

Danny was clinging onto the front seat for dear life. He relaxed his grip. Patrick was clutching the upholstery in the Rambler. Danny took several quick breaths. "Yeah."

Patrick didn't let go of the seat. "I'm shaken up a bit but I think I'm okay."

"What was that?"

Danny turned towards Mr. Pym. "Don't know but I was talking to Patrick and whatever it was ran off in front of me mighty fast. Man, it was big."

The teacher opened his door. "Hang on a sec. Don't get out of the car." He stepped out and cautiously moved to the front of the Rambler.

*

Jeeze, what was that? I gotta keep my wits about me or the boys will be scared.

Mr. Pym fumbled in his vest pocket for his packet of Camels and his Zippo lighter. He lit the cigarette with trembling fingers.

I shouldn't have had so many beers last night before I went to sleep.

He took several long, deep drags on the cigarette and cautiously moved to the front of the Rambler.

Nothing. The chrome was in place and there wasn't a dent.

There was the stink of something musky and something else but his mind was too busy trying to calm himself down to think of what. He dropped to his knees and peered under the car. He could feel the gravel of the road rubbing against his legs through his pants.

No leaks. Pipes and hoses look fine.

He popped the hood over the engine.

No cracks on the engine block. Everything looks good. He closed the hood with a dull thud. Mr. Pym went around the car and continued looking into the forest. He saw Patrick and Danny tracking him as he walked around the car.

He was definitely puzzled.

Pym got back into the car, banged the door shut, and shifted the car into "D" for drive. "I think we are okay, gentlemen, and that is pretty odd considering it felt like we were hit by a train."

He crushed his cigarette out in his ashtray. The boys pinched their noses.

"Sorry guys. I am trying to quit."

The Rambler turned around on the road and continued home.

*

"I'd just as soon not stick around to see what hit us, guys."

Patrick saw Mr. Pym jam on the accelerator.

Danny was getting excited. "Wow, might have been Big Foot?"

"No idea, Danny. We'll sure have one great campfire story to tell though. Patrick maybe you did see a bear after all." They all tried to force a smile. Danny already started lounging back in his seat up front. In a few minutes it would be like it never happened.

Patrick wished he had a weapon.

The bear just wanted to let Patrick know that he was around. Patrick wasn't sure what else the bear wanted.

He dug his fingernails into the seat of the Rambler and scanned the forest.

Wrong Indian

Jan and Ron discovered Winfield blocking the door to the interrogation room. He was leaning nonchalantly against the concrete post that was to the left of the glass door.

Leon Winfield looked like everybody's stereotype of a government man. A crew cut. Short-sleeved white shirt. Blue pants. Blue tie. Polished black shoes. Bland.

Before Winfield had joined the Immigration Naturalization Services (INS) he served twenty years in the Marines as a drill sergeant. Rumor had it that somewhere along the way towards the end of his military career he worked under Ollie North. Leon Winfield showed about as much concern to the illegal immigrants he was responsible for as he might have shown to the Sandinistas. Ron muttered an obscenity. Jan tried to silence him with her eyes.

"Hello, Mr. Winfield, to what do we owe the pleasure?"

Winfield rocketed straight as if somebody was forcing an enema inside of him. "Dr. Brighton, Detective Adamovich. I was just waiting for your detectives to conclude their interrogation of your witness before I escort him on a plane back to Ecuador."

Ron rifled a glance through the glass door. He jerked is left thumb up pointing towards the room. "But that is the Mexican Indian we brought in."

Winfield attempted a laugh but it came out a snarl. He was enjoying this.

"No sir, apparently you've deduced that he is the wrong kind of Indian. He is not Mayan. He's Jivaro and here illegally. He's not Mex. Sorry, doctor."

Jan chose to ignore his baiting. She despised prejudice. In her background there was talk that she had great grandparents from Mexico. Winfield knew it.

Ron was boiling.

Jan casually moved closer to Winfield and looked him straight in the eye. "Mr. Winfield, if he is a witness to a murder, we can hold him. Something we should know?"

Winfield lightened up a bit. "Possibly. I personally don't think that he'll be much use to you. There is always the possibility of extradition later on. Of course, you know these types. Once he disappears in the country he'll vanish and you'd be sunk. I want to know what's going on with this case."

"You a detective now, Leon?"

Winfield's jaw tightened. He hated being called by his first name.

God, Jan thought, please shut Ron up.

"What Detective Adamovich means, Mr. Winfield, is that it might be easier to keep him here until we get this investigation resolved."

"I'm only doing my job, Doctor. We're seeing more and more transients from the Americas enter through Mexico these days and it's like adding insult to injury, if you know what I mean."

"Well, at least he didn't call me 'Beaner Lover'", she thought to herself.

"I get you, Mr. Winfield. May I please go in and see if I can get anything to add to my research in this case?"

"Was in there myself already. He's not a talker. Probably scared to death. Keeps saying you wouldn't understand."

"Someone like you probably wouldn't. Stop stalling and move," Ron moved around Jan and poked his finger directly into the INS man's chest.

"Ohhh look who just committed battery on a federal agent. Should I press charges now, tough guy?" Leon Winfield grinned like a jackal.

Ron retreated.

Jan touched Ron's arm. She was afraid Ron was playing right into Winfield's trap. Winfield and Ron knew each other back in Miami and it was hate at first sight. Men like Winfield liked to test people's limits, push all the wrong buttons and watch the fun. Ron wondered at times if Winfield really was transferred to L.A. because of his no-nonsense, bullyboy treatment of illegals or because Winfield got bored with Miami and wanted Ron to play with.

He also was fishing for juicy stuff to help build his career. Fine, I'll toss him a bone.

"Gentlemen, please. We've had a long and tiring time of this. Ron, we can trust, Winfield."

She paused for dramatic effect wearing a smile. "Right now this case is so hot it is scalding my teetas. I need to know what could have torn apart and suffocated several human beings."

Winfield's brows shot up.

Good. He's interested. Maybe he can help us. Good doggy, Leon.

"If you could let him stick around for awhile without letting red tape get in the way, I will not only keep you appraised with what happens, I will make sure you get shared credit if we solve this case. It will have to be on the q.t. though."

Jan could have sworn he clicked his heels together like a Nazi. He was adjusting his stance. "Thank you, doctor. I'll keep it quiet." He shot a look at Ron. "I'm glad there is somebody around here who is civilized enough to deal with this professionally. FYI, it is the Jivaro who wants to leave."

Jan nodded her head in agreement. "Makes sense".

"He's a scared pussy." Winfield stated.

"Wouldn't you be?" Ron asked.

Now you've done it, Ron. He's been waiting for an opening like that. We'll never get in that room while you two play, "Who has the bigger gun?"

"There isn't much that can scare me anymore. Between the fighting I've seen over in my time in the service and after I –"

"Can you give us civilians a break? I heard all this back in Miami and I was sick of it back then. I was in Nam and I don't wear it on my sleeve like you do, Winfield."

"You'd have never lasted a day in my unit, Detective."

"Got that right. I'd have been court-martialed for shooting my commanding officer the first day in action."

Jan raised her arms and formed a "T" with her hands. "Time out. Ron, I think that we've taken up enough of Mr. Winfield's time."

The two men glared at one another like Hulk Hogan and Mr. Fuji, two of Patrick's favorite wrestlers..

Jan leaned forward and peeked into the room. The room was a plain, white room with a long oak table. Seated at the table were three men. Two of them were detectives. The detectives were dressed in suits and looked fresh from the Academy.

Everybody is looking younger to you these days, huh, girl?

The third man was the Indian. He had to be in his fifties. He had what looked like half a torn book in front of him. It was the man Jan saw getting into the squad car back at the crime scene. The detectives were apparently asking questions and judging from their body language, they all seemed friendly. She mentally tried to place the detectives. Jan didn't recognize them.

"Who are the detectives?"

"Ross and Ramirez. Ramirez is fluent in Spanish. Ross gets by."

There was a Sony micro cassette recorder running on the table. Two tiny tapes were stacked next to it. The Jivaro slowly turned and looked at Jan.

Their eyes met. She felt a slight jolt.

This time it felt stronger than when she felt it earlier. The Old Indian turned back towards the detectives. One of them saw what had happened and approached the glass door. He turned the knob.

"Dr. Brighton? I'm Chuck Ross. Want to come in now? Hey, Ron."

"Chuck."

"Sure." She motioned Ron to the side. The INS man soaked everything up with spongy, grey eyes.

"Okay?" Ron asked.

"Just startled."

"Need me in there as well, Doctor?"

"Not right now, Mr. Winfield. Let's go, Ron."

She entered the room. The door closed behind itself. The detectives rose and astonishingly, so did the Jivaro.

Well-mannered guy, if nothing else. Ross handled the introductions.

"Uh, Joe, this is Detective Adamovich and Dr. Brighton".

The Indian extended his hand. Ron shook it and looked at the Jivaro.

The man's face was heavy with lines of age but there was a crispness to his skin that reminded Ron of the good health that he saw in some physical fitness geezers who worked out at Muscle Beach. His handshake was firm for a guy who was afraid of talking about what he had seen.

Injun Joe turned to Jan and shook her hand. She smiled. He then lifted up the papers in front of him and handed them to Jan.

*

Jan took the papers from the man and as soon as they were in her hand found herself transported to a room that was completely white.

Inside the room was Injun Joe and a young good-looking man wearing a toga.

"Jan Brighton? Welcome to part of the book "The Lowerworld". My name is Leonard and we don't have much time."

Sinks

Los Angeles
Jan and Patrick's house 9:40 AM

The blue water spirit (also known as an ata) had received instructions to wait and capture the boy in case its brother water bear spirit failed. It bubbled out of the garbage disposal in Jan's kitchen.

It started appearing as if something was backing up out of the sink.

It took a vibe. Finding that the prey wasn't there, it started to enter the room.

Slowly, it started filling the stainless steel sink with gallon after gallon of its transparent blue body. It leaned over the sink and sized up the kitchen like a thick, droopy rug.

A stove. A table. A refrigerator. A microwave oven. Cabinets.

The ata took another vibration reading of the room.

There were no living beings present that were a threat to it. Its victims were not here so the ata could prepare itself.

There was some fungus growing underneath the floorboards.

Some bacteria in a piece of chicken in the refrigerator.

A spider was under the sink.

But not for long.

The spider was attaching webbing to the curved pipes. The ata allowed itself to slip underneath the cabinet and engulf the spider.

The spider struggled. The water spirit had slipped itself between the creature's pores, covering the bug's joints and entering every orifice it could find. In a few seconds, the spider had been suffocated.

The ata withdrew from the curled-up corpse and examined the products under the sink.

Liquid plumber. A plunger. A large economy can of Lysol. A spray container of Fantastik.

A bottle of window cleaner.

The ata formed a hand and unscrewed the spritzer from the top of the window cleaner. The spritzer cap came off and the ata let it drop to the floor.

The bottle was half-full. It allowed a portion of itself to flow into the container until it was filled to the rim. It gently replaced the spritzer back on the window cleaner sprayer and screwed it tight.

The spirit went from room to room leaving pieces of himself hidden in case the boy would return.

When the boy returned, he would drag the child down into the Lowerworld for his master.

Lowerworld and Injun Joe

Jan was staring at the man and Injun Joe.

"What is going on?"

"You are inside part of the book called 'Lowerworld'. I am one of the guardians who was part of the book and sadly the book has been torn. This book was being escorted to the Library in Northern California when there was a truck wreck."

The good-looking man walked next to Jan. "Part of this book was torn. A man making his way up to California found it. He is obsessed with revenge. The other part, this part, managed to make it into the hands of this nice gentleman here."

Joe smiled. "Can I have a drink now please?"

"When you get out of here, Dr. Brighton, please give this guy a drink."

"Uh, sure."

"I don't have much time – my power is weak because the book was torn and the bulk of the energy is in the other piece. You must recover the other piece of this book. You must also find the book that was escorting this one to the New Alexandria Library."

"This can't be real."

"Oh it is real. You better watch out for your son, Patrick, as well."

"Huh?"

"There are powerful magical forces and guardians from the book that must be stopped. Put these pages in your pocket and don't let them out of your sight."

Jan blinked.

She was back in the room with the other detectives with her hands on the pages. The Jivaro was smiling at her.

The man was letting go of the pages of the book.

"How long was I gone?"

"Huh?" Ron asked. "You just walked into the room."

"Oh, right, right. Injun Joe, what did you want to drink?"

"Anything as long as it has booze in it."

She tried to discretely fold up the paper pages as she asked the detectives to get the man a proper drink.

Jan and Ron asked some basic questions. Injun Joe just ran errands for the guys and his story was pretty much what he said in front of the other detectives.

Jan didn't quite know what to do or think at this point.

A detective brought back a bottle of Whiskey and a paper cup. "Sorry we don't have any glasses."

Injun Joe poured himself a drink and sighed.

"Did you have any more questions for me?" Joe asked Jan directly.

"No, I think we are finished. Thank you. Thank you very much."

Ross and Ramirez escorted the man out of the room. Winfield was starting to ask questions.

All of a sudden there was a thud and people yelling. Jan and Ron ran outside.

Lying on the floor several yards down was Injun Joe. Ross and Ramirez were bending over him. Leon Winfield was barking orders to uniformed officers who were running down to see what was happening.

"Get an ambulance. Hurry!"

Jan ran over to Injun Joe.

He was on his back and a trickle of blood was seeping from his mouth. Ross moved aside. Ron approached Winfield.

"What is it?"

"Damn cleaning people. There was some murky slop water on the floor and the guy slipped on it."

Sure enough, there was a small dark puddle underneath the man and some of it was on his clothes.

The liquid appeared to be drying up and evaporating at an incredible rate!

Jan couldn't believe her eyes. She took Injun Joe's pulse.

"Forget the ambulance. He's dead. His neck's broken."

"Crap."

*

The water spirit finished slithering back into the bucket in the janitorial closet. It sent a signal back to his partner stationed at Jan's house that it had taken care of a loose end.

Shop Talk

Ron's Desk 10:30 AM

Ron was grateful for small favors as he brushed his hair back with his left hand. The fact that Winfield was gone was a plus mark on an increasingly negative criminal investigation. He finished typing his report on the IBM Selectric III and muttered a curse that he forgot to change the correction ribbon.

The Chief wanted an interim report and Ron was doing this one by the numbers. Everybody plays detective when they think it can help them win an election.

"What if that guy had any relatives here? They could sue the city for beaucoup bucks. Find our janitorial contract and make sure that we are off the hook on this one. Then talk to our departmental attorneys to make sure."

You're all heart, Chief.

Jan had examined the dead man and prepared the papers concerning his death. She was consulting with her team to see if they had anything to add to the puzzle of this case and the unfortunate bad luck of the late Injun Joe. Ron wanted to get her away and grab something to eat with her but they just didn't have time.

He typed over his mistake and yanked the form out of his typewriter. When the hell will they fix my PC and bring me back into the Twenty First Century? Ron Adamovich motioned to a uniformed officer that was walking by. The officer, an attractive brunette, approached his desk.

"Can you get this to the Chief for me? I saw you walking towards his office. He's crawling on my ass for this one."

The officer nodded sympathetically and took the form from Ron's hand.

"Thanks! I owe ya one."

Time to check on the janitors.

It was standard operating procedure (sop) that whoever had the contract for the cleaning of this station had to have been run for clearance in order to get bonded. There was information that might be thrown out that shouldn't be seen by the casual civilian or the not-so-casual attorney trying to get his jailbird client off the hook.

Ron got up off his swivel chair and headed for the accounting department. Checks had to be cut for this janitorial service, too.

Ron strolled past an elderly man in a green sports jacket arguing with a burly detective. Stevens, Ron remembered.

"I wanna pay my pah-king ticket."

"Sorry, sir. You will have to go to the Clerk of Courts for that. See the address on the ticket? That is where you have to go."

"But I'm here aw-red-dee."

Ron nodded at Stevens as he walked by. Stevens rolled his eyes and smiled. He was having one of those days, too. Ron thought about his early days writing tickets. The one place you didn't want a parking ticket was L.A. The just-a-second Charlies who failed to put that quarter in the meter would always get nailed. So would the Red Zone Ritas that didn't realize that even though you initially couldn't be arrested for not paying your ticket, you could be levied a whopping penalty which would surface at the most embarrassing times, like vehicle registration time!

Ron reached the glass door that was stenciled "ACCOUNTING". He pushed the door open and approached a series of desks lined up neatly four-by-four in the room. Four attractive Latino women were working the desks. Ron approached the first desk. He picked up the scent of Aviance perfume. The middle-aged woman at the desk was opening envelopes with a long letter opener. She made a face at Ron.

"Ladies! Mira! It's the Great Detective! He has come to grace us with his presence."

The women looked up and made "oohh" and "ahh"ing noises. Ron had to admit to himself that he loved it and that was one of the reasons he walked over to accounting instead of phoning over. Besides, he needed a break from all the death around him.

"Ahh, Carmen, ladies. You spoil me. How is life?"

She made a "thumbs down" motion with her thumb. "The people in Auditing lost some records they took from us and they are yelling at us that we are at fault. What can I do for you, handsome?"

"Can you dig up who has the contract for maintenance of the station?"

"Si".

Ron wondered what had happened to the janitor who had left the floor wet when the Jivaro walked through the hall. That water evaporated incredibly fast.

Too fast.

Maybe it was something supernatural.

Carmen was busy at a microfiche viewer replacing blue pieces of fiche in and out of the viewer. She finally yanked a piece and with a dramatic snap of her wrist, she turned off the viewer.

"Not on fiche." She walked over to a brown filing cabinet and yanked open the middle of three drawers. Ron's mind wandered back to the janitors.

The bucket, he thought.

If the floor was wet, the bucket should have been in a closet nearby. Why didn't we look for it earlier? We were too busy with Injun Joe...

He made a mental note to look for the bucket on his way back to the desk.

Carmen pulled out a manila folder. "Voila. The on-line system is down so we had to look for the hardcopy." She sashayed over to Ron and handed him the folder. The outside of the folder had a sticker with a green band on it with the words. "STATION MAINT" typed on it.

Ron opened the folder.

"The cupboard is bare," he said.

Carmen looked inside. "Damn those auditors. They probably forgot to tell us they took files from here, too."

"Who can I talk to in Auditing to look for the contract, cancelled checks or anything that can help? In fact, is there anybody here who knows of any of the cleaning people or the name of the firm?"

The ladies shrugged their shoulders. "Now that you mention it," the blonde named Rosa said, "I don't remember seeing anybody cleaning these halls during the daytime or night for the last few months. It is always clean though."

Carmen scribbled a name and an extension on a yellow post-it note. Ron picked it up.

"Try this, home." The ladies laughed.

Ron whirled, "Thank you, girls, I love you, too."

They waved good-bye and Ron realized that he could be as charming as the next guy if he wanted to.

Ron walked down the hallway to the janitorial closet.

There were no signs on the door and it was pretty unremarkable. He moved closer.

As he approached the door he suddenly was overcome with a severe case of anxiety.

"Stop that," he told himself.

"What's eating me? It's a well-lit hall and people are walking by every other second."

A black detective rushed by as if to emphasize the point. He was carrying a small box with folders in it.

Ron was uncomfortable. He felt himself sweating under his armpits. His knees started to get weak. He took a few deep breaths to relax. He pocketed the yellow sticker he got from the girls.

"No matter how I feel, I WILL open this door," he told himself.

He pulled himself together. His fingers reached beneath his jacket. The 9mm automatic he was looking for was safely nestled in its holster.

"Great, I will look like a total chump shooting a mop. Am I a man or mouse? Come on and squeak up."

Ron took another deep breath.

He opened the closet door.

It was dark. He fumbled for the wall switch. He clicked on the light. There was a sink, a mop against the sink and a bucket with a wringer inside of it. There were tiny droplets of water by the wheels of the bucket. The water level was about a third full.

Ron relaxed and turned off the light. He shut the door. He'd come back and get prints off the bucket if it weren't too late.

Who knows how many cops handled it moving it back and forth if it were in the way of something in the station halls..

Ron went to look for Jan feeling better that he had faced his fears.

After all, it was just a bucket of water.

*

The bucket of water behind the closed door bubbled.

Across town, the water spirit in Jan's house received the message.

Soon.

Circus

Jan's Office 11:00 AM

Jan saw Ron coming out of the hallway and entering her office out of the corner of her eye. She was reading some of the reports that her staff had prepared for her.

He looked like he's seen a ghost.

"Maybe a book ghost?" She asked herself silently.

Detectives Ross and Ramirez were next to her. She was in the process of telling them that her team hadn't found anything new. She made a mental note to ask Ron later what might have spooked him. Right now she had other things on her mind.

The phone rang twelve times when she tried home. Nobody answered. Patrick was old enough to take care of himself. She could always leave word with the neighbors to take him out for a pizza or some junk food until she got home.

In trying to determine what kind of animal might have been loose that killed the drug dealers, Ross and Ramirez had traced all the major circuses. All of them were out of town and pending answers from carnivals; they had the rundown on all of their animals. Jan's call to the LA Zoo yielded nothing except the assurances of the keepers that the animals were "all in their places with bright shining faces."

She held back from inviting the zookeepers to come to the morgue to see some of her "bright shining faces".

They had one lead. A local amusement carnival, the kind hired by churches, Elks and fraternal societies in the city was not far from where the murders happened. She wanted to go along with the detectives to inspect the animals herself.

"Ron, we tried calling the Samson Circus. It's been in town for the last week at the Church of the Lady, about twelve blocks from the scene of the murders."

Ross stroked his chin, "We tried calling them and they got damn evasive."

Ron was regaining some of the color back in his cheeks from being frightened. "So let's go check 'em out."

*

They arrived at the carnival at ten after eleven. The detective had word that the owner of the carnival was parked in the Winnebago that was by a pay phone at the church. When their unmarked Fury pulled into the parking lot, Jan saw the carnival people already entertaining the mid-morning crowd. There were four Winnebago motor homes and two semi-trailers parked in a corner of the lot by the pay phone. There was a small midway of about half a dozen carny booths and about four rides: a Tilt-A-Whirl, a Flying Spyder, a Merry-Go-Round, and a Ferris Wheel.

"Nothing for really young kids," she mentioned to Ron.

"I guess we go that way," Ron said as he pointed to a sign that read "SAMSON'S CIRCUS". She saw several moms lifting their toddlers out of their strollers to see several animals and a man in a clown suit performing.

Ramirez had been driving and he had parked the car on the street. Ross and Ramirez walked over to the first Winnebago by the pay phone. Ross knocked on the door.

A bald man with liver spots on his head chewing an unlit cigar stuck his head through a drape and peeked out the window of the camper. The drape flopped against the glass and in a second, a voice grumbled behind the door to the Winnebago.

"Yeah?"

" 'Morning. I'm Detective Ross of the Los Angeles Police Department. Are you the owner of this carnival?"

"Lemme see some i.d."

The man cracked the door opened. Ross flashed him his badge. The door opened all the way.

The man was in his fifties. He was wearing an old T-shirt with a wolf grinning over a pie with the inviting message, "IF IT SMELLS GOOD, EAT IT." The man must have been taking the shirt at face value since it barely covered his overhanging gut. He was wearing some torn blue jeans and had on a brand new pair of Adida clone shoes.

Jan had walked over with Ron.

The man rolled the unlit cigar around with his mouth and finally pulled it out with his left hand.

"I'm Turner. I own the carnival. What can I do for you, Detective?"

"This is Dr. Brighton from the coroner's office and Detectives Ramirez and Adamovich. We are looking for any kind of animals that you have. Any wild animals like lions, tigers, bears or wolves? Also, why didn't you answer the payphone you are parked next to when we tried to call you?"

Turner stepped out of the Winnebago. He closed the door behind him. Jan caught a glimpse of rotten pears on a counter.

Turner motioned for them to start walking over with him towards Samson's Circus. "I was worried that you were after me because of the kid the other day."

"What kid?" Ross asked.

"This kid rides on the Tilt-A-Whirl and decides to climb out of the seat while it was moving. He broke the restraining bar. He wasn't too bright."

Jan looked at him attentively. "Was he hurt?"

"Naw, the ride was coming to a halt but I was afraid that he talked to a lawyer or something and his parents would try and sue. I think he majored in stupid in school to begin with, if y'ask me. Say are you like 'Quincy', lady?"

"Something like that. The reason we are here, Mr. Turner, is that we need to know if any animals got loose last night."

"Y'mean like dogs, monkeys or bears?"

"Yes, especially bears."

Turner smirked.

They got closer to the circus. It was more of a dog show. There were three trained poodles jumping off of the clown's knees and one bored looking chimpanzee sitting on a director's chair. The mommies were saying things to keep the kids interested but even the toddlers were starting to look bored.

"The gyps use to own the circus."

Ron leaned forward, "Pardon me?"

"The gyps. Gypsies. I bought it from them down in San Diego when the owner was arrested for an aluminum siding deal he was scamming on the side. Me, I don't have any troubles with the police. Nosiree."

They approached the back entrance of the wooden hut that housed Samson's Circus. He opened a back door and yelled inside.

"Samson, c'mere."

A gangly-looking man in a tank top and shorts who looked like he was no older than sixteen came to the doorway. He reminded Jan of Patrick's friend, Danny Hunsinger - only older.
"Samson, Jeff ain't got the bear on stage and these folks are police. They want to

know if any wild animals got loose last night."

Samson grinned. He was wearing braces.

Jan thought to herself that they couldn't be doing that badly if he could afford braces.

"We only got us five poodles, a monkey and the bear, Boris."

Ramirez smiled, "Can we please take a look at Boris?"

Samson grinned. He looked knowingly at Turner. "Sure. Follow me."

They walked to a cage that was boarded up inside the circus façade. Samson produced a key and opened a padlock that was holding the door to the cage closed. It stunk of animal droppings. Samson tugged the rusty cage door open. Inside on a bed of hay was Boris.

Boris was a brown bear possibly five and a half feet tall wearing a muzzle. He was lying on his left side. Flies were buzzing all around him as if he were a piece of feces. His fur was falling off. Large red patches of skin were exposed and if it weren't for the movement of his chest, Jan would have thought that the bear was dead already.

"No, I don't think ole Boris was out and running around lately," Samson grinned. "He's been sick this way for the last few weeks. Had a vet look at him and he thinks it is bear cancer. If he don't get better in a week we are gonna have to be puttin' him to sleep and send him to bear heaven."

Ron was mad.

"I'm calling Animal Control. We're going to cite you. What the hell were you doing, charging admission to see the bear while he was suffering? Can humans contract this cancer, too? You're endangering those kids outside."

Turner frowned. "What kind of place do you think I am running here?"

"One in violation of several health ordinances, Turner. This isn't safe. Are your rides secured?" Jan added.

Turner shrugged. "You've got problems with me? Write me up. I'm finished talking to you. Y'know, I'm outta here in another day so why don't we let things be and I will make it worth your while."

Ross was getting mad, too. "I'll haul your carny ass downtown right now if that was a bribe, you pig."

Turner looked at Samson. "I didn't mean any kind of bribe. Did you think that was a bribe, Samson?"

"Naw. I didn't think that was a bribe. Did you, Boris?"

Boris opened his mouth. A greenish, infected discharge oozed out of his mouth.

"Arrggh", Ron growled.

As they were driving back to the station, they saw the Animal Control van pull up to the carnival. Ron and Jan were sitting in the backseat. "I don't see how they can get away with it, Ron."

Ron turned towards Jan. "They figure they can bribe the locals were they go. The organizations that hire them turn a blind eye when they see that it helps them raise money. Shame too since I loved carnivals as a kid. Nearest thing to a circus some of them might see in their lifetime as well."

"Do you think they will pay the citations and fix things?"

Ross chimed in from the front. "They better. We can pass the word around that the carnival is bad news to any church or charity group that hires them. That'll get them to either clean up their act-"

"Or leave," Ramirez said as he glanced in the side mirror.

The real truth was that carnivals, like Turner's, did grease the wheels of local law enforcement and somehow managed to stay in business. There were no closer to solving the case than before. Turner's carnival was ruled out. That poor bear couldn't have mauled the flies away from its head let alone several armed drug dealers.

Ron looked at Jan.

"I'm going to get on the people in Auditing when I get back and we'll nail down who the janitors are and see what is going on with them. Strange that the records for the contract, the checks are missing. Also, I haven't honestly seen anybody cleaning the building and it has been clean."

Jan thought for a second. He was right. The building was not only clean, it was cleaner than she had seen it in years and she didn't remember seeing any janitors or cleaning crew as well.

Her thoughts drifted over to Patrick.
She wondered if he had gotten home yet.

Pit Stop

Lucky Seven Truck Stop Noon

"Oh boy! A burger would be good now, huh, gentlemen?"

The Rambler pulled off of the highway up some tarmac into a huge truck stop. A giant metallic sign roared LUCKY SEVEN GAS. Patrick had never seen so many trucks stopped before. He was impressed. With so many truckers (and truckers – who were badazz dudes, huh?) the bear wouldn't dream of bothering him here. There was a gas station that looked like it could service twenty cars and trucks at the same time. Currently, there were two tanker trucks and a Corolla being gassed up.

Mr. Pym parked the Rambler between a Ford Bronco and a VW Rabbit. He opened the door and stood up. Danny and Patrick got out of the car. They stretched their tightened bodies.

"Was I sleeping again?"

"What do you think, Hunsinger?"

Mr. Pym smiled. "Let's grab something to eat. We can zip back into town after that. Then you can grab some sleep when you are back at your homes."

They closed the doors to the Rambler. Danny had to shut his twice because he got the seat belt stuck the first time between the door and the frame of the car. Patrick smelled the diesel fumes from the trucks. He felt the rumbling of the big rigs as they drove on and off the tarmac. They were loud, too!

His stomach grumbled.

Mr. Pym and the boys trudged past some puddles. Patrick stopped and looked at one of them. It was a gasoline puddle. Patrick could smell the gasoline fumes and he didn't find them altogether unpleasant. He was getting hypnotized by the rainbow reflection in the puddle until Danny rabbit-punched his shoulder.

"Ouch."

"C'mon, Pat. Stop huffing gasoline."

"I wasn't huffing gas!"

"Look where Mr. Pym is!"

Patrick straightened himself out. Mr. Pym was a good thirty yards ahead of them. The boys jogged to catch up with him.

"What did you see, Pat?" Mr. Pym asked.

"Nothing, I was tired and I was looking at the colors in the gas puddle. I wasn't trying to sniff gas or anything."

"I know what you mean. The way the light produces a rainbow reflection is very interesting and if you are tired it is very hypnotic."

"Yeah." Patrick was impressed. Mr. Pym caught on right away to what had happened. Should he tell Mr. Pym that he really thought that the bear was out to get him? The car had driven fine since the accident in the woods earlier. Mr. Pym didn't seem to make much out of it so maybe it wasn't such a hot idea to bring it up again.

I'll bet Mom or Ron would believe me.

Ron listened very closely to Patrick whenever he talked. Ron was the person who warned Patrick about the initiations.

Yeah, I bet Ron would believe me. Mom would too because she was, well, Mom.

They approached a pair of sliding glass doors that opened when the overhanging sensor picked them up. A short man with a cap advertising SHELL walked out the doors. The trio entered the building activating the sensor just as the man was leaving causing the doors to remain open.

A universal sign with a silhouette of a man was hanging over a door. Its female counterpart was across the room in the wide hallway to the restaurant and gift shop.

"Pit stop," Hunsinger said as he pushed open the door to the men's room. Patrick and Mr. Pym followed him in.

The restroom was surprisingly clean and smelled of disinfectant. It reminded Patrick of the bear and he started to tremble. He went into a stall, unzipped his pants and relieved himself.

How many miles was he holding that for?

The faucets were those push button kinds that release by themselves and either pops up too soon leaving your hands soapy or keep running forever. He squirted some pink soap from the dispenser. Gently he rubbed it between his fingers.

It felt squishy.

Using his elbow, he depressed both buttons and stuck his hands back and forth between the two streams of water. There wasn't a lot of pressure in the pipes so he wasn't splashed.

It was the quick release kind of faucet. Patrick found he had to repeat the process three times to get his hands free of soap. He wiped his hands on one of the paper towels that were stacked on the counter. He exited the bathroom.

Patrick was happy to be away from the cleaning smells and he started to relax. First phase of the pit stop complete, he thought.

Cleaning accomplished, time for refueling.

Dan surfaced from the restroom. His hands were in his pockets. Patrick sized up the gift shop that was next to the restaurant.

The gift shop was a giant enclosure filled wall-to-wall with the knick-knacks, souvenirs and items a tourist or trucker might want to buy on the open road.

Time for that later.

The restaurant was what really got Patrick's interest.

Mr. Pym emerged from the restroom and took a second to get his bearings. "Food is on me, guys."

"Thanks, Mr. Pym."

"You don't have to, Mr. Pym."

"Quiet, Patrick, before he changes his mind."

Mr. Pym motioned for them to move towards the food. "Just don't tell the other scouts or I'll have to feed the whole troop on the drive home from the next campout."

The restaurant consisted of bright red and white booths that were probably constructed in the nineteen fifties. A transparent plastic corridor surrounded them. The food was served cafeteria style and the boys went first as they followed the corridor along to the food.

At the smell of desserts, Patrick realized how hungry he was. He grabbed a tray and some plastic utensils. He leaned forward and plucked down a piece of apple pie. Danny joined him inching down the line scoping out green salads (which he took one of), soups (El Paso, gracias), and the hot plates. Danny had the chili plate and Patrick stuck with a hamburger and fries. Mr. Pym followed and took a burger, too.

They told the bored-looking, young brunette at the cash register that Mr. Pym would pay for their meals as they drew Mountain Dews from the soda fountain.

It was Danny who picked the window seat for them.

"Thanks again, Mr. Pym."

"Yeah, thanks, this is great."

Mr. Pym sat opposite them in the booth. "You're welcome."

Patrick and Danny devoured their food like wild dogs. Try as he might, Mr. Pym just ate a little slower than they did.

I guess we all were starving, Patrick thought.

Mr. Pym wiped his mouth. "I give it another hour or two depending on traffic till we get to town."

"Mr. Pym, what do you think about that thing in the woods?"

Crap, Danny. Don't start.

"Maybe it was a bear. Maybe it was a log. Who knows? At least we got a yarn to spin, huh, guys?"

Patrick forced a smile. He looked down at his empty plate. He looked at his pie and didn't seem to be hungry anymore.

"Not gonna eat that, Tenderloin?"

Patrick pushed his plate towards Danny. Danny lifted the pie and replaced it on top of his empty dishes.

The pie was history in seconds.

Mr. Pym took a sip out of a cup of coffee that he had gotten for himself. "Give me about five minutes and we'll take off. I just need to kick back for awhile."

Good. Patrick wanted to be alone. "Can I go look at souvenirs, Mr. Pym?"

"Sure."

"I'm going to go look at some of those rigs outside, Mr. Pym."

"Danny, don't talk to any strangers and don't get in anybody's way, okay?"

"Ah, I'll be all right."

Danny picked up the food trays and bused them from the table to a garbage can and onto a conveyor belt. Patrick separated from Danny at the entrance and entered the gift shop.

Danny called after him, "I'll sniff some gas for you."

"Bite me", Patrick responded.

Danny laughed. He went outside.

Patrick entered the gift shop and wanted to hide. He went to a revolving rack that had comic books on it. He picked up a copy of Detective Comics.

It was two months old. He had it and he had read it.

Patrick leafed through the pages, trying to calm himself. He replaced the comic and turned to look at the magazines. There were a variety of Road and Track, Field and Stream and People magazines stacked next to True Detective and American Astrology.

The cashier, a woman in her fifties was reading an old copy of Weekly World News. She called over to him.

"Hey, kid."

"Yes, ma'am?"

"Want a free book? Some trucker found this out on the road and I can't sell it. No charge."

"Uh, okay."

The woman reached under a counter and pulled up a book. She handed Patrick the book, "Leo and Woofy's Day At the Beach."

Patrick was compelled to take the book.

"Thank you."

Before he could open the book, Danny came running into the gift shop. "Patrick," he exhaled, "You gotta see this."

The cashier looked up from the article DEAD MAN'S HEART STARTED WITH JUMPER CABLES! She scowled at Danny. "No running in the store please."

"Sorry. Ya gotta see this."

Danny led Patrick to the glass door by the entrance. A tanker was parked about one hundred yards away and men were running all over trying to stop a long hose connecting to the ground from leaking.

"They were filling the gas tanks underground and the hose underneath, y'know' that big, ungodly thick one? Well, it's one that connects the tanker to the ground and it got a leak. What a mess! Better not light a match after all, Tenderloin."

"Huh, Do we have enough gas in our car?"

"Dunno. We better check with Mr. Pym."

Patrick gazed out the window and froze. To the left of the tanker truck, about eighty yards away, he saw a large, furry creature skulking between some parked cars.

More Bad News

Jan's Lab 12:15 PM

Jan was examining some blood under a microscope when it happened. She felt a chill and a jolt similar to what she felt when she first opened the pages from that torn book. She was very aware of her surroundings.

And worried about Patrick.

No sense in continuing until I find out what's up with him. She never felt this worried about him before. He was able to take care of himself and, yes, she was over-protective.

But something was up.

This book business and this case were putting me over the edge. I'm getting as paranoid as a speed freak.

She tried phoning home but nobody answered.

Mr. Pym wouldn't leave him at home all alone. Plus Patrick would call as soon as he gets in. She tried phoning a neighbor. No answer.

Jan considered herself a person who believed in God but her practical experiences made her think that God helped those who helped themselves. She believed in God but she also believed in other – creepies, for want of a better word.

Many of these strange creepies had manifested themselves before her in her years as a doctor of forensics and before. She witnessed a person who was clinically dead pop back to life five minutes later after a man practicing Santeria came to remove a curse.

She had come to the conclusion that it was the belief that the human mind and spirit puts individually and collectively over the years into something that adds power to it."

Well, belief or otherwise, it was the "creepies" in between God and man that gave her headaches. Like murders.

She replaced the phone on her desk as Ross entered. He looked tired and Jan could sense that he didn't have anything good to say to her.

"More bad news?"

Ross looked like he lost his best friend. "We've just got a couple more murders, m.o. similar to the ones earlier this morning."

"I'll be ready in five minutes. Where's Ron?"

"He's on his way with my partner. Ramirez knows somebody in Auditing and the two of them were shaking some cages trying to find out who has the maintenance contract and cancelled checks for the building's janitors. I'm looking for the tie-in since there is the strong possibility that Injun Joe was murdered, too. That, as you know, isn't as far-fetched as that sounds. I called Ron right after I got the report over the radio."

"Any details I should know about?"

"It's sketchy at this point."

Jan decided to pack some of the photographs she made of the murders from this morning. If there were any bite marks, she could make plaster molds to recreate the assailant's teeth. If she could do the same of any of the clawing she might pin down what kind of animal it was. Like she tried to do earlier.

She didn't hold her breath on that one.

Jan had Myra Lewis run the claw marks down for her in the morning. They were nowhere near anything they could cross-reference. Myra had also researched several volumes of pictures of animal prints.

"It's like these prints were out of a kid's fairy tale from some mythical monster," Myra had said.

God, I hope not, Jan thought.

Six minutes later, Jan and Ross were driving across town in the van. They had raised Ron on the radio.

His voice came in clearly. "My ETA is about five minutes, Jan. Police have secured the area."

Ross was holding the microphone in his hand.

Ross depressed the button on the mic. "We'll be there in about five, too."

Static. "Copy that. Drive safely."

The roads were a mess. In the lunch hour traffic, people sometimes went a little nuts on the Los Angeles streets and freeways. Reports were coming in over the police band for at least a half a dozen accidents in the last few minutes.

Must be the pollution, Metro rail detours or people hating to go back to school or work.

They passed a series of orange cones and the two-lane street they were on narrowed down to one lane. A man in a hardhat and orange vest motioned them down the street slowly with an orange flag.

"Metro rail, bah!" Ross exclaimed.

At the rate the city seemed to be dragging its feet with the train system, the new public mass transportation lines wouldn't be finished until Patrick was old enough to retire. She was sorry to hear that the Santa Monica trolley project was stopped. She loved trains. Gilberto, her ex, surprised her one-year for their anniversary and took her on a cross-country train ride. He had packed some champagne, cheese and crackers for the ride.

She admitted to herself that she had some good times with her ex-husband.

Back to work. She drove past the remaining cones, as the street became two lanes again.

"It's about another three blocks from here." Ross said.

She was sitting next to the torn pages of the book. She heard a voice in her head that sounded like the voice she heard earlier saying, "Your friend Ron is going to be at the next intersection."

Jan stopped her van at the next intersection. She slowly started moving down the block, freaked out from hearing voices in her head.

She drove slowly passing two houses as the neighborhood gave way from residential to commercial. Some zoning commissioner must have been paid off, she thought. They slowly reached the intersection.

The Fury that Jan was in earlier pulled up to a stop sign. The headlights flashed. Ramirez was sitting at the wheel and Ron was in the passenger seat.

"There's Ramirez and Ron", Ross said.

Jan started sweating. A strong feeling of dread enveloped Jan.

"Your son is in danger too," the voice said, "but don't worry, he is being watched over."

The Fury turned the corner and Jan pulled up behind it.

"Who are you?" Jan thought to herself.

The voice answered her in her head, "I told you already, I am pages from the book, "Lowerworld" and you need to find the rest of my missing pages or everybody is in great danger."

Out of Gas

Lucky Seven Truck Stop 1:00 PM

Mr. Pym had joined the boys by the entrance to the restaurant to watch the recovery operations being conducted by the tanker. The men finally stopped the flow of gas from the rig. They had changed hoses. The gas was flowing into the huge underground tanks. Mr. Pym turned to the scouts.

"Ready?"

"Yeah," Patrick was barely able to talk.

"Do we have enough gas, Mr. Pym?"

"As a matter of fact, I don't think so. We have to fill up, Dan."

Patrick had lost sight of the bear. He saw him moving around some detached trailers that were lined up in the back of the parking lot. Mr. Pym's Rambler was parked on the other side of the lot so he thought he was safe.

Plus since he touched the book he got from the truck stop, he was able to relax for some reason.

"C'mon", Mr. Pym started walking to the Rambler.

There was a line of cars and trucks starting to back up at the pumps. The station must have been lower than they thought on gas for the lines to be so long.

That meant that they had to wait a long time until they got gas.

The bear could do a lot of damage in the meantime to Patrick and to the truck stop.

The trio marched to the Rambler, Patrick eyeing all around him to make sure that the bear couldn't get at him. Everything appeared safe. Mr. Pym produced his car keys. He unlocked the doors for the boys to get in.

"You can ride shotgun, if you want."

"Thanks, Dan. I will."

"I'm gonna try and go back to sleep."

Mr. Pym opened his door and slid into his seat. With a bang, he shut the door and the guys did the same. He turned the key in the ignition. The gas gauge lifted to "E" and did not rise any further.

"I better pull into line before it gets any longer."

Pym turned the ignition key all the way and the car started up. Dan rearranged some sleeping bags in the back and leaned his head against the rolls. Patrick checked out the cars to his left.

He saw the bear clawing at the muffler underneath a VW bus.

Patrick heard a voice in his head, "Patrick, as long as you keep the book close to you, you and your friends will be safe."

"Who are you?"

"I'm Leo. This is Woofy."

Patrick heard a dog bark in his head.

He looked around and realized that nobody else was hearing this except for him. He clutched the book. The book was unimpressive and frankly looked kind of old to Patrick.

The Rambler lurched forward and sputtered. Patrick looked up. The car rolled forward. The gas tank was empty.

"Dang. Sorry, guys. Our luck ran out. Danny, up and at'em. We have to push the car over to the line."

"Is it okay if I stay in here and steer?" Patrick squeaked with his voice.

Please say yes he thought to himself.

"Okay. Slide over to the driver's side and get ready to work the brakes, too."

The scoutmaster got behind the Rambler. He started leaning against the tailgate. Danny held the passenger door open and was leaning against that. The lot was straight so they didn't have to worry about the car rolling one way or another. Patrick glanced quickly to see what the bear was up to.

It was gone.

"Hey! Watch it, Pat!"

Patrick looked in front of him. He had veered to the side.

He saw he was about to collide into the side of a flatbed truck covered with cages. Inside the cages were squawking chickens.

He hit the brakes. The car stopped with plenty of room.

"Squawk – squawk – squaaaaawk".

Mr. Pym moved to the front of the car and planted himself in front of the hood. "Put 'er in reverse."

Patrick did and the car started rolling backwards.

"Hold it."

Patrick braked.

"Turn the wheel to the right and line it up behind that station wagon. Be sure to brake it so they have plenty of room in case they have to back up."

"Steady, Patrick", Leo said into his head.

Patrick gripped onto the steering wheel for dear life. He lined the car up. He could see a kid sitting up in the back of the wagon staring at him. The freckled face, redheaded kid was getting closer. Patrick hit the brakes.

"Good. Put it in park."

He did. By Patrick's counting, the Rambler was sixth in line. There were two cars already at the pumps. A Chrysler LeBaron and a Yugo. Behind them were a Chevy Impala, a red Porsche, a station wagon and finally, the Rambler. The flatbed with the chickens pulled next to the Rambler.

"Squakkk".

Something was spooking the chickens.

And Patrick.

Mr. Pym got in on the driver's side.

"Guys, I'll need both of you to push it in slowly while I steer it."

Patrick reluctantly got out of the car. He tucked the book underneath his shirt in the back of his pants.

The air smelled of formaldehyde.

"Squa-awwk".

Patrick looked at the flatbed truck. The bear was nestled in the center of the truck. An open cage was lying next to him. The bear was chewing on something. Feathers flew in the air.

It was the neck of a chicken.

Patrick turned towards the Rambler.

"What am I going to do?" he thought to himself.

"Grrrrrrrr", Woofy growled in his head.

"Easy, Woofy. We can't leave Patrick." Leo said. "Patrick, keep focusing on moving the car forward."

The LeBaron and Yugo pulled away from the pumps.

The line slowly moved forward.

"Let's push Patrick."

Danny was on the driver side of the car pushing. Mr. Pym was pushing from the driver side, too. He jumped in and applied the brakes as the car began nosing too close to the wagon.

Patrick was concentrating on his hands. He had pushed well enough but he felt the life draining from his fingers. He was frightened and felt like running away from the truck stop.

"That's just what it wants," Leo said. "We wouldn't stand a chance against it on foot right now. Woofy and I are still weak."

"Maybe we can get some help from others."

Patrick yelled at Danny. "Dan, check out those chickens."

"Noisy licks, aren't they?" The scout grinned.

"What's that at the center of the truck?"

"Dunno, looks gnarly though – did you see all that blood?"

It was hard now for Patrick to see in the center of the truck. The cages had appeared drawn tighter together. The only thing visible was the chicken that had been decapitated. It flapped its wings for a few seconds out of some automatic galvanic response.

"Cool-o! Did you see that headless chicken, Pat?"

Even Mr. Pym looked up trying to discover what all the commotion was about.

The cars behind the Rambler honked. The Impala and Porsche had crept up to the two gas pumps. There was a gap of about twenty yards between the scouts and the back of the station wagon. The boys pushed. The car rolled slowly behind the wagon. There were newspapers bundled and stuffed in the back of the station wagon. Patrick was getting nervous and was having a hard time keeping his food down. He burped, re-tasting his lunch in his throat.

The driver of the chicken truck was a hairy, thin man who was chewing gum. He opened the door. The man took big strides to the back of the flatbed and climbed in.

"What's all the racket, girls?"

"Squaw-wak!"

Patrick heard the man grumble an obscenity. A truck rumbled past and he couldn't hear anything over the sounds of the car engines and the wheels roaring on the ground.

"Patrick," Leo warned, "I wish there was something we could do to help that man but we just aren't strong enough yet."

Patrick peeked back.

Thankfully, the man returned from the back of the truck and started inspecting the tires. Relieved, Patrick turned towards Danny. Danny was staring at him.

"Y'awright?"

"I think so. I guess I am seeing things. You know that bear that hit the car earlier? Or what I thought was a bear?"

"Uh huh?"

"Don't think I am too much of an ass but I think I saw it on the back of the chicken truck over there."

Danny made a face. "Must be those fumes that you huffed earlier, Tenderloin?"

The wagon moved forward. Patrick gripped on the side of the Rambler and pushed. The car inched up behind the wagon.

They were finally in the service area.

An attendant came over to Mr. Pym as he got out of the car. Even though it said self-service, several attendants were helping people pump gas to speed up the lines.

"Ten of regular. I also ran out back there so I may need a little directly in the carburetor." The scoutmaster went to the front of the car and popped the hood.

"Can I fill it?" Danny asked.

"Sure."

Patrick got in the car as Danny pumped the gasoline into the tank. Mr. Pym and the gas station attendant played with the carburetor. The attendant admired the Rambler.

"Your car looks fine, mister. Good job keeping it up, too. There should be no problem starting it up."

Patrick started relaxing as Danny replaced the hose on the pump. Pym got back inside the Rambler.

He turned the key.

The engine caught the first time and started.

"All right!"

Danny got into the back. Within three minutes they were back on the highway darting to Los Angeles.

*

Back at the truck stop, Jon Brandstetter, the driver of the chicken truck scratched his head. The forty year-old hauler couldn't figure out why the flatbed truck was tilting so far to the left. He had checked the tires and the cages.

There was that large brown lump in the back of the truck that stunk like the devil's testicles. He didn't examine it any further because he thought that his shock absorbers were screwed up.

Maybe it was some rabid dog.

Brandstetter pulled out a pump shotgun from the back of his seat. He decided to go back for another look-see.

"If you are a mean annie-mule, you are a dead annie-mule," he said to nobody in particular.

He climbed back up on the flatbed and started moving cages around.

There were dead chickens everywhere.

The clucking and squawking of the terrified birds was starting to get to him. He moved behind two large cages.

A brown paw grabbed him and pulled him to the ground. Jon Brandstetter was pinned to the floor of his flatbed under one paw. His gun was awkwardly angled away from him.

He couldn't even reach the trigger.

Another paw was holding down a chicken while a pair of huge sharp jaws closed over it causing blood to splatter all over the pinned trucker. The bear looked directly at the trucker eye-to-eye.

The last thing Jon would remember before the bear would kill him was a soft, friendly voice scolding him.

"Shame on you, silly. Do you like to be disturbed when you are eating?"

Myra's Lunch

Jan's Lab 1:45 PM

Myra Lewis had turned off her microscope, gone out to get lunch and returned to her workstation. She stretched her neck.

"I need a massage. I hope Vince isn't busy after work."

She tried dialing Vince.

His line was open. She got his machine.

Either he's out on an audition or out dating some hootchy actress.

She couldn't figure out why a talented, good-looking woman like herself was dating a loser like Vince.

After waiting for the beep, she spoke. "It's me, Myra. I'll be working late tonight so give me a call if you want to get together later on."

She hung up the phone.

He makes me laugh.

Well, so does Bugs Bunny. That's no reason to date him, either.

She unwrapped the taco she had bought. She took a bite. It was greasy, hot and delicious.

After things slow down at work, I'm going to give serious thought about continuing or discontinuing my relationship with Vince.

She placed the taco down.

There were some files she had to check the animal prints with. Everybody would be returning back into the lab at any minute. She loved her job and Jan was a tough, but fair boss.

At review time, Jan had taken good care of her financially speaking, and she looked forward to her career growing while working for Jan. She still liked to work alone. The nature of forensics was that everything be done in collaboration.

Sort of like building the atomic bomb.

She usually went to lunch by herself and more often then not, used the lunch hour to take advantage of the feeling of extra space she had by herself in the lab.

Nobody was in the room with her now. Some of the assistants had gone to help with the latest killings (more work) and some were still at lunch.

Over in the corner of the room was a bucket of brackish water. There was no janitor nearby. Myra could have sworn that she didn't hear the door open to the lab.

Who left that in here?

That could be dangerous left there by itself and unattended.

She walked over to push the bucket off to the side.

The door to the lab opened. Some other lab workers came back in. She turned towards them. She smiled. Myra turned back towards the bucket.

It was gone.

She must have been seeing things.

Maybe she'll hold off breaking off with Vince.

All this stress must be getting to her.

Dead Coyotes

East Los Angeles 2 PM

The office building, the newest one in the area, was surrounded by squad cars. It was the same office building, which Jan had heard of from some of her Latino friends. Its tenants were some of the sleaziest businessmen in East Los Angeles. The tenants of this building couldn't afford Century City, Beverly Hills or Santa Monica (yet). Instead, they buried themselves like ticks on a dog in this new structure in the heart of the Spanish speaking part of Los Angeles.

The police had their share of busts here. Tenants came and went in a matter of weeks. These people were con men and they prided themselves on successfully beating their raps. Many of them boasted to their arresting officers exactly what they were doing. They were cocky and sure of beating their own prison sentences.

This was the place of the new mutilations.

The building stood six stories tall. The murders were committed on the sixth floor. Two uniformed officers: Peters, a tall, dark male and Nolans, an attractive black woman were standing in the doorway.

The three detectives put their badges on their belts. Jan clipped her i.d. to her collar. They were led in swiftly. Ron started the talking.

"What have we got here?"

Nolans, who was an inch taller than Ron, answered him. "Two coyotes. Brothers. Ferdinand and Carlos Delgado." She was very serious.

A light of recognition seemed to appear on Ramirez. "I heard of 'em. They were always dodging the Border Patrol. We could never get anything on them that would stick."

The way a coyote worked was very simple – in theory.

The coyote stationed himself in Tijuana and let word out that he was able to smuggle people across "El Norte" – to the North. Peasants, the rich, the innocent and the wicked, anybody who for whatever reason, couldn't immigrate legally to the U.S. would approach the coyote. For a steep price, he'd arrange for safe passage to California, a safe haven and a job waiting for you.

If you were lucky enough to get an honest coyote.

Some coyotes took your money and killed you at the border. Others would separate the families and take any attractive women for themselves for prostitution. More often than not, even if the coyotes were honest, the living accommodations waiting for somebody coming to America were one step below the worst imaginings of poverty. The work waiting for you was usually in the fields or busing tables – if you were lucky. Maybe a cleaning position. Making the journey itself was very dangerous with the Border Patrol sometimes getting trigger-happy and the traveling conditions usually cramped and infected.

The coyotes' office consisted of three desks, two swivel chairs, a couch and several filing cabinets. It looked half moved into. Jan saw blood all over the walls and walked over to two forms covered with sheets. The room stank of formaldehyde.

"It smells of our killer."

She bent over and lifted one of the sheets. The body underneath was unrecognizable except for a wallet in a plastic bag that was lying next to it. A dirty driver's license read "Carlos Delgado".

"You officers did a great job securing the scene," Jan said.

They smiled.

Jan looked at claw markings. There was also severe tissue damage. What killed them first – the shock of the clawing or the heart being quartered?

Jan settled into work mode. She set up her kit and wished she brought Myra with her.

The three detectives went through the file cabinets as some more of Jan's assistants arrived.

*

Jan had lost track of time. She looked at her watch. It was 4:30. Her assistants had finished packing themselves up and had left. Ron had a grim look on his face.

"A dollar for your thoughts, Ron."

"These Delgado boys were real gems. Take a look at these. Ross?"

Ron motioned for Ross to move closer.

Ross was carrying a stack of manila folders. Each had a typewritten note card attached to it. He handed the folders to Jan. She opened one.

Inside was a picture of an attractive Mexican girl. She couldn't have been more than twelve. There was an address scrawled on the bottom of the picture in black ink.

She was posing in her underwear.

Jan handed the folders back to Ross.

She had seen enough and could imagine what was in the other files.

"They were running the girls through to make them hookers."

That sickened Jan more than anything she had ever encountered on the tables in her morgue. How could men be so cruel that they take advantage of somebody else's trust, exploit them and sometimes kill them?

These were children, dear God.

Ron looked at her like he knew what she was thinking. "It almost makes you glad that these bastards got it, y'know?"

"Every indication points to the same m.o. that we found in the crack house, Ron. The coyotes died of shock to their nervous systems by loss of blood. It's hard to tell if they felt anything. They have been gutted."

Ron fumed. "I hope they lingered."

Nolans, the policewoman, approached Ron. "I think we may have somebody who saw something."

Ron's features brightened. "Who?"

"A tenant down the hall. Some attorney said that he heard something."

Jan looked at the carnage around the room.

Dear God, how could somebody NOT hear something?

Ramirez and Ross produced some plastic bags filled with guns and spent casings. Ron continued to talk to Nolans and walked with her to the doorway. She examined the plastic bags that the other detectives were holding. The guns felt warm, even through the plastic.

"Both weapons were discharged completely. We found some holes in the wall and the ceiling and we were able to dig out the slugs. No luck in connecting with whatever it was that got them."

The room was getting stuffy. Jan was tired and the smell of formaldehyde and of the bodies was just too much.

Keep at it, Jan, whoever did this is still out there.

"What if it was the spirit from the book?" she thought to herself.

Somewhere in Los Angeles, a man, a woman, or a group of people was plotting some more murders. She felt it. Something about the pages from the book she received was convincing her that no matter what conventional means she'll try to solve it with, she'd never get close.

How do I stop spirits from a book?

Ron came back to Jan. "I'm having Nolans bring this attorney over to us. I also had Peters put in a call for a couple more back-ups. I don't want anything happening to this witness. Just in case something is being leaked from inside the department."

"Good idea. Ron, after all that has been happening, we are in agreement that Injun Joe was murdered too and it wasn't a coincidence, right?"

"What do you mean?"

"She means, she thinks it was a spook, you know, a ghost," Ramirez said. His face was like a stone. He said it matter-of-factly without any humor. The case was getting to him too!

"If it is a ghost it is out of my pay grade. I just want to take as many precautions as possible. We have another immediate problem that might mushroom," Ron said.

"What's that?" Jan scratched her forehead.

"Our attorney friend is looking to make a name for himself. He's already telephoned the Times, the Herald and half a dozen local Spanish papers. He is planning on giving a press conference."

"Great. Can I sedate the man?"

"He called them about ten minutes ago, so with any luck, our back-ups will keep the press out and we can lock this one down before it gets out."

Jan knew it was probably too late for that. Word was already out on the street and the Latino community would soon demand some explanations (and rightfully so). How come two armed men were mauled in their offices? Why aren't the police doing something to apprehend the madmen responsible? After the hassle several months ago about response time from the police being slower in high crime areas in Los Angeles, she could hear the media cries of prejudice being raised again. The truth is that the police are over-worked and can't be everywhere at the same time.

Whatever this thing was, she suspected it could be wherever it wanted to be, whenever it wanted to.

She looked at the plastic bags that had the guns.

They reminded her of packing a lunch for Patrick. A sandwich, an apple and dessert all wrapped in plastic in a lunch bag.

She prayed that Patrick was okay.

*

About sixty-five miles outside of Los Angeles, Patrick had the feeling that his mother was thinking about him. He wished that he had tried calling her back at the truck stop.

The bear was not following him.

At least, not on the busy highways that poured into Los Angeles.

Patrick knew he wasn't out of danger.

Some feeling grabbed him and he trembled.

"It's a spirit from the Lowerworld book, Patrick," he heard Leo whisper to him.

"Spirits?" Patrick asked aloud.

He felt his spine shiver with warm, tingling tickles racing up and down his back.

Mr. Pym turned briefly towards him. "What was that?"

"Uh, nothing. Just talking to myself."

"Spirits? As in ghosts?"

"Who ya gonna call? Ghost-busters!" added Danny.

"Yeah something just crossed my mind."

"It was a dark and stormy night in the spooky, monster-filled skull of Patrick 'Tenderloin' Brighton."

"Knock it off, Hunstinker, or you'll be seeing stars in another minute."

Danny chortled. He sat back in his seat.

What was getting into Patrick? What made him say that?

"He's a knucklehead," Leo said. "Patrick, the bear is a spirit bear that cannot be killed with bear traps, shotguns or normal weapons."

Patrick felt Mr. Pym staring at him.

"I guess I dozed off and had a nightmare."

Mr. Pym turned back to the road.

"How do I fight something like that, Leo?" he thought to himself. He pulled the book out of the back of his pants and opened it up.

It was an old children's book. Nothing remarkable looking. The colors on the illustrations of the little yellow-haired boy and his black Scottish terrier had started to fade.

In comic books, there was always a super hero who had magical powers that fought spirits and demons. He wasn't a Doctor Strange or a Doctor Fate fan. How come all the magical guys in comics had "doctor" in their name? Did it make them sound like experts or something?"

"Patrick," Leo continued softly, "I am still weak otherwise I could show you that you have it within you to do things like the characters you read about in your comic books. You need to be strong and brave."

"I'm scared", Patrick thought. "I don't know if I can be brave."

"Well, if you can't be brave, then the alternative is that you will be dead," Leo whispered matter-of-factly.

Bedtime

The Sanchez Residence
Los Angeles, California   4:30 PM

"Anna, will you please take a nap for now?" Iris Sanchez was upset. Naps or early bedtimes were rough on her.

"I want to hear a story, por favor, Mama, just one, pretty please?"

Iris was tired. She was in her twenties and had worked a hard shift as a waitress at Coco's. Enrico, her husband, was still working two jobs as a security guard for two different companies and the bills were finally being paid.

Bless Our Lady!

She looked at Anna. The little girl was sitting up in her bed, her brown eyes sparkling, her lips pouting. She was wearing a Raiders T-shirt (her Papa's), and had all her stuffed animals in bed with her.

She looked like one of the angels in the prayer books from church.

Madre Dios. What a pain she was today though!

When Iris picked Anna up from her Grandma's house, Anna had wanted to go play Ms. Pac-Man at the Seven-Eleven. Fine. One game, Anna. Three games and seventy-five cents down the tubes later, Anna was asking to rent "Princess Bride" from the video shelf.

Children. God, isn't there a way you can bless bambinos so they are born potty-trained, quiet when you ask them to be and blessed with knowing the value of a dollar? When they got home, Anna, threw a fit because she couldn't watch Princess Bride during her early dinner.

That girl sometimes...

Okay, she wants a story? I'll give her a GOOD one.

"One story, tu savy? One."

"Yeaaaaaa!" She clapped her hands like a pair of cymbals.

"First settle down."

How many sugared churros did Grandma give you today, chica? You are wired!

Anna fluffed her pillow and leaned against it. She cuddled with the Roger Rabbit doll that she got as a birthday present.

"Once upon a time, there was a magical kingdom, far beneath the land. In this magical kingdom, there was a beautiful princess."

"Like me, Momma?"

"Si!" She smiled at her daughter's beautiful eyes.

The room was small, but well stuffed with children's toys. Sure, she shouldn't have gotten pregnant when she did but Enrico was a good man. He did the right thing and married her. She glanced at the window. The shade was pulled and the drapes were closed. She hoped the setting sun wouldn't keep her daughter awake.

"If you want to wake up later to see Poppi, you need to relax now. Where was I? Ah, the princess had everything in the world. She was only five years old."

Her little eyes widened. "Like me!"

"Si, mija! Like you sweetheart."

Thank God I didn't have any kids at thirteen like Rosalinda did. How did she make it out of high school?

"Her mother, the queen, said to her, 'Chica, you can have anything you want in the world, but, you have to

sometimes wait for it.' The princess was
very spoiled and said, 'But I want things
now!' The queen smiled and said, 'Very
well, but sometimes if you get things
right away, they are not worth it
because you can't appreciate them.
You may be better off waiting for them.'"

She paused for effect. Anna was
looking at her spellbound. Good good.

"Well, this princess asked for the
biggest, cutest stuffed toy in the whole
world. People all over the kingdom
searched high and low until this old
wizard said he could make her one, only
if she could wait a couple of years. This
chica said, 'No, Senor Wizard, I demand
you make me this cute stuffed toy NOW
or I'll ask my Mommy to cut your head
off pronto'. She could be a really holy
terror, y'know?"

Anna giggled.

Ah, did I catch a small yawn after
that giggle? I sure did. Bueno.

"So this wizard delivers a huge wrapped box to her castle the next day. The princess demands that her guards open the box and inside is this giant, brown teddy bear. She orders the wizard to make it perform for her. He tells her, 'But your Highness, I need more time to perfect my magic.' She says, 'Now!' He shrugged his shoulders and commanded the bear to perform. The bear comes to life, okay? He grows these big, gnarly teeth." She flashed her teeth for emphasis.

"And these big, big claws." She extended her pink fingernails.

Too bad one of them had chipped.

Anna giggled. "More Momma, this a good story."

"The bear was actually a monstero and ate two of the guards. Gobble, gobble. Like Ms. Pac-Man."

She tickled Anna for emphasis. "The princess screamed, 'Senor Wizard, stop it. I was wrong. I should have waited. Make it go away.' He bowed and waved his magic hands and poof! The monstero disappeared."

Anna was closing her eyes. "So this princess apologized to everybody and said next time she would wait and get a present that would be worth waiting for. The moral of the story is that sometimes it is good not to rush things."
Anna's eyes popped open.

"That was great, Momma. Again. Another one, another one."

Girl!

"No, you need to take a nap if you want to wake up and see Poppi when he gets home from work. Remember; be like the princess in the story. Wait and you will see. I'll have another story for you tomorrow night. Don't rush things."
"But I want a story now!"

"Go to sleep, Anna. Don't be like the girl in the story!" She leaned forward and kissed Anna. The little girl grabbed her around her neck and hugged her tightly. She giggled.

"I was joking, Momma. I'll be good." Iris straightened herself out. She inspected the night-light in the corner of the room and clicked it on and off and back on again. She closed the closet door and turned off the silent mercury switch on the wall. The switch glowed a warm, cozy, yellow in the dark.

"Night, Momma."

"'Night, Anna. I love you."

Finally. I love you Anna but my feet are killing me. I have to soak them. Dancing at Stella's was killing her. Iris had gotten into her robe and filled a small basin with hot water. She was about to put her feet in when she heard a scream from Anna's room.

She ran to her daughter.

"What is it honey?"

She turned the light on. Anna was sitting up in her bed and crying.

Everything else looked normal. She couldn't have fallen off her bed.

"The monstero."

"What monstero, Anna? Did you have a bad dream so quickly?"

"No, I saw his shadow on the drape. The monstero."

God, why did I have to tell her a monster story? You can be so stupid at times, Iris.

"Let Momma look, okay, Anna?"

"No, Momma, he said he'd eat you!"

"There are no such things, Anna."

"It's real. I'm scared."

"It was only a story, honey."

What was out there? A burglar?

She scooped Anna up in her arms and ran into the kitchen. Iris grabbed a meat cleaver and returned to the bedroom. She went over to the window. She peeked out the shade and drapes.

The window was facing the right-of-way between her house and the house next door. Light was shining in from the street. She could see the paint peeling on the blue house next door. Other than that, there was nothing out of the ordinary.

"Whatever it is darling, it is gone. Want to try to sleep in Momma's room?"

She nodded.

I'll carry her back when she falls asleep. Crazy nightmare. She replaced the cleaver in the kitchen and carried Anna over to her bed. Anna bounced once as Iris dropped her on the mattress.

"Honey, did you really see something in there or are you making this up so you can sleep in Momma's room?"

Anna started crying. "I saw the monstero, Momma. I saw its shadow on the shade."

"There is nothing there now, sweetheart. Maybe somebody walked in the alley." She might call the police and ask them to send a patrol car to the area.

"It scared me Momma."

"Well, it is gone now."

"It said, it would get me, get you, get the boy and then get the dead guy who was trying to control him and the water spirits."

This was getting silly. Unless somebody in the alley overheard my story...

"Stop it, Anna. You mean to tell me that the bear was in the alley and said that it would come back?"

She smiled meekly.

The room smelled of formaldehyde.

Iris' bedroom closet door opened.

"Boo! You tell a great story, Iris," The bear said as he opened his mouth revealing rows of long, sharpened teeth.

It wouldn't be long before two more victims would be found for Ron and Jan.

Another Witness

Delgado Offices – Hallway 5 PM

Either the thermostat was controlled automatically or somebody turned up the air conditioning. It was freezing. The blasts of cold air eased the smell. Mr. Stone didn't seem to be bothered by the smell or the cold.

J. Avery Stone was standing in the hallway directly underneath a vent. Stone kept glancing at his wristwatch. Other than that he was imperturbable. He was black-haired, with a thin moustache. He was wearing a beige, polyester suit.

Jan could have sworn she'd seen him before.

"You look very familiar to me, Mr. Stone."

The attorney smiled flashing several gold fillings. He puffed up like a rooster at sunrise. "It must be from my commercials on TV."

That was it.

Too much stress? You may be entitled to Workman's Comp benefits.

Sexual harassment on the job? That's against the law!

Need citizenship? Arrested for DUI (Driving Under the Influence)?

Call Stone, an attorney that you know is as solid as a rock.

In Jan's eyes, he was your basic, full-service, ambulance-chasing, anything por-a-dinero television attorney.

No wonder he called the press!

"Was he planning on running for Mayor as well?" she mused to herself.

Ron had a pen and paper. Ross produced a small notebook from his jacket pocket. They were getting ready for Stone's statement. Stone glared disapprovingly at them. "Hurmph".

Stone cleared his throat.

Ron winked at Jan. He put on his best "Officer Friendly" smile.

"I'm sorry, Mr. Stone, the reporters are not allowed to enter the building. If you want to talk to them, you'll have to do so downstairs, outside. For now, we would appreciate it though if you wouldn't."

Stone's dazzling television personality was nowhere to be seen. It was like he turned off a switch!

"Unless I see a gag order, I'll do as I please. Get on with it. You have questions for me?" he commanded.

His voice had that bored, mock-aristocratic air to it. Like some viceroy who was being inconvenienced by the civil serfs. Ron wasn't about to let him off the hook. He kept on smiling.

"Mr. Stone, in your own words, what happened earlier?"

The attorney cleared his throat again. He began like he was giving a speech before Congress. "I was sitting in my office preparing some briefs for a court appearance tomorrow when I heard some screaming from down the hallway."

Ross and Ramirez were appraising the man. It was Ramirez who made the next move. Ramirez leaned forward and lightly placed his hand on Stone. Tactful body contact, she thought.

"Do you have a secretary, sir?" Ramirez asked quietly.

"I do. Balbina Ysidro. She has been with me for two years. She was out today for the holiday while I was catching up on some paperwork. I went towards the door to the guys' office. Didn't know them personally, but they seemed decent."

"Did you ever have any business dealings with them before?"

"They wanted me to set up, ah, uh, an international corporation for them. Didn't get all the details."

"So you didn't know them personally but you were going to set up a company for them?"

"Met them through my secretary. They talked with her. I knew them only from hellos in the hall, things like that. Anyways, I was by their door when I heard gunshots. I ran back to my office. It seemed like the prudent thing to do. I telephoned the police. May I go downstairs now?

"Just a couple more questions, Mr. Stone."

"If you must."

Jan couldn't believe this guy. He was probably involved in God knows what kind of business deal with the coyotes and was shafting them to cover his own worthless butt. Ron will need to get probable cause for a court order to search his records.

"Did you hear them say anything to anybody?" Ron asked.

"If you call cries and pleas to God for help conversation, yes."

"Do you know anybody who might have wanted to kill them?"

"No."

"Were there any other tenants on this floor or in the building who might have heard anything?"

He raised an eyebrow as if to sentence Ron to the guillotine.

"That's your job, detective. I don't know who else is in the building. Why don't you and your partners start knocking on some more doors?"

"Thanks for your time, Mr. Stone."

Stone added condescendingly, "I know my job and my responsibilities as a citizen, Detective Adamovich. I phoned the police. Do you know your responsibilities?"

"Yes, I do sir. Don't leave town and I am getting a court order to see your files."

"Do what you have to do."

With a flourish of his arms, the attorney left. Ramirez followed him out a short distance. Ross moved closer to Adamovich. "You are lucky he didn't say he'd sue you for police brutality."

"He's lucky I didn't book him for impersonating a human being. I'm sure he's trying to figure out what to spin this to the press as. Ramirez will keep an eye on him and correct any inaccuracies."

"Is this an election year?" Jan asked. "Let's go."

Jan and Ron were walking back to the coyotes' office when they saw a door ajar.

The voice from the pages from the book spoke in her head. "Wasn't that door closed a minute ago?"

Jan stopped and walked slowly over to the door.

Ron picked up on it as well. "I could have sworn that all the doors were closed a few minutes ago."

Ron led the way slowly.

Gripping his gun with one hand and grabbing the doorknob with the other, Ron swung open the door.

It was a cleaning closet.

The interior of the closet was spotless. A clean, white mop was perched against a wall from the inside of a brand new, silver bucket. Jan thought you could have eaten out of it. A white, antique porcelain sink was above the bucket and a wrapped bar of generic soap sat on a mirrored soap dish.

"Ron, this room is too clean."

"I know, I know. We'll get somebody up here to dust the closet. Come with me, I don't want you to stay up here alone."

She nodded.

Jan was uncomfortable in the cleaning closet. There was a feeling of emptiness and draining inside of it. Despite its order and lack of dirt it felt too sterile.

Like her morgue.

Ron grabbed Jan by her arm. He pulled her away from the room.

They scrambled for a uniformed cop and posted the officer in front of the closet.

Motioning to Jan, the two of them went to look for a lab technician.

Evidence

Jan's Office 5:55 PM

The bucket and mop found inside cleaning closet were dusted, photographed and replaced. There didn't appear to be any finger or paw prints on the cleaning equipment. Jan was busy with Myra at work on one of the samples from one of the bodies back in her office. She peered at a slide of tissue through a microscope.

There were the same slashings as were on the other victims.

No other blood other than the deceased's and faint traces of window cleaner.

The evidence indicated something weird. Something supernatural for lack of a better understanding.

"When all else fails, step back and take a break." She snapped off the illuminator on the microscope. Almost automatically she peeled off her gloves.

She sighed, "Let's take five, Myra."

"If you don't mind, I'll keep at it."

"Whatever you want. Just don't exhaust yourself."

Myra is a good worker but I wish she wouldn't push herself so hard. Jan went back to her office. She closed the door. She and Myra had talked about the need for a couple of neck massages. Her ex-husband gave great massages – when he wanted to.

In the early days of her postgraduate work she looked forward to her back rubs. She'd work like a dog with her studies and keep house for him. Latino machismo values die-hard. Her husband got his freedom and a clean divorce. She got exclusive custody to Patrick, her career and resumed using her maiden name.

If he really loved Patrick and Jan he would have tried some attempt at compromise.

Enough bad memories.

Jan had drained her cup without realizing it.

One of those moods, girl.

Better concentrate harder.

Another lab man found nothing. Not even a trace of fiber to suggest that gloves or anybody wearing any clothes was even in the utility room.

Jan started writing up her report.

There was a knock on the door.

"Come on in."

Ron entered her office.

They had separated briefly while Jan had continued with her analysis. Ron had made sure that two policemen were stationed outside her lab at all times. She felt better that the officers were there she knew that if push came to shove, they wouldn't fare well against any spirits.

"Your son might fare well against the spirits," a voice from the Lowerworld book said in her head.

Jan freaked and tried calming herself down.

She picked up the phone. She jumped.

"Ron!"

Ron was standing there.

"I think I am losing it."

"I hope not. Anything?"

"Uh, no. Bodies had several incisions of latitudinal and longitudinal direction and multiple bruises. Lacerations are the same as the prior cadavers."

"Nuts."

"What did you get?"

"The mop and bucket were standard issue from any Smart and Final Iris Wholesale store. Whoever did this is good. There is no trail whatsoever."

The book pages talked into her head again. "Wait, he will come to you."

Jan trembled.

The Janitor

Jorge Longrunning's Warehouse 5:45 PM

Jorge Longrunning rubbed his eyes with his fingers. He opened the door in the back of his warehouse and stood in the doorway. It was getting late. The clouds had started covering the sun.

He took the pages of the book, Lowerworld, which he found from that car accident he witnessed and went back into his office in the back of the old, white warehouse. He closed the door.

His tall, six-foot figure barely fit into his office cubicle in the corner of his warehouse. That didn't bother him. He pulled a manila folder out of the top drawer of a metal desk. He opened the folder and pulled out a clipping from the Los Angeles Times Metro section.

There was a picture of Jan and Patrick.

He smiled and replaced the article back into the folder. The story was a human-interest piece on the medical examiner after she appeared to speak in front of a Future Careers for Women hosted by a Beverly Hills civic group.

Jorge was lucky that he found his half of the torn book from the Ancient Library. Evidently, the book was on it's way to a library up north and was under some sort of spiritual escort when the truck that was carrying it got into an accident.

Jorge was hitchhiking and had hopes of making it back to Peru when he found the torn pages. They were enough to begin to get his revenge.

Unfortunately, they weren't enough.

The fact that the coroner woman had the other half of the book seemed almost like a cruel joke to Jorge. She was the woman who did the autopsy on his son.

Jorge took his set of pages of the book, Lowerworld, and closed his eyes.

He concentrated.

He relaxed and found himself tugged forward as if by an invisible chain.

When he opened his eyes, he saw he was speeding past stalactites and stalagmites jutting towards him like some giant set of carnivorous, rocky teeth.

He was inside the book. He had learned his way to map the pages and get a degree of control from the book.

Jorge was always in awe of the different colors and structures of crystals that he would see in the caverns as he would fly by. Light came from the rocks themselves in the cavern. A twinkling, white light appeared at the end of the cave. It rapidly became the opening into a clearing.

He willed himself to slow down.

The janitor saw sunlight illuminating a flat landscape.

A big brown bear was waiting for him.

"What do want from me now?" The bear asked.

Jorge smiled. "How was your trip?"

"Okay."

"Show me."

The bear lurched.

Images from the bear's point-of-view materialized in front of Jorge. He saw the man with the chickens being devoured. He saw an image of a terrified Patrick staring at him from the Rambler.

Jorge froze at that scene.

He sighed.

That face. That face. Like his son.

"Go back to the boy and follow him till I tell you or the water spirit to bring him to me."

The bear growled, "I'm tired of listening to you. You shouldn't even be in here."

"Enough!"

The bear lunged at Jorge and raised a paw.

"I am stronger than you!"

Jorge concentrated and bear's paw became transparent and passed through him harmlessly.

Jorge grabbed the bear by its neck and the bear roared. "I yield."

"Do as I say and do it now."

The bear turned around and raced off.

Jorge Longrunning's hatred and desire for revenge made him very strong. The pages of the book he had were controlled by Jorge's will power and imagination. Being a janitor, Jorge could create spirits that were natural Peruvian creatures and make them out of cleaning chemicals or in the case of the bear, the preservative chemicals that were placed in his dead son.

He planned on trying to get his dead son back to life.

*

The bear was created from the energy from the book. The book decided that it didn't accept Jorge as a master or as somebody who should be welcome in the Library. Unfortunately, this man had will power that activated the energies in the ancient book. This book, like others from the Ancient Library of Alexandria, was imbued with the ancient life essences of long dead scholars. After thousands of years, some of the books just wanted to be left alone.

Like this one.

This particular book was hiding in South America when the Library found it.

A guardian spirit book was escorting the book back to the New Alexandria Library in Northern California when it tried to escape. It ended getting itself temporarily torn in half.

One half is now in Jan's hands.

This half was in the hands of this revenge filled fool.

The book pages talked to the bear spirit that Jorge had conjured up.

The pages told the bear spirit to kill Jorge Longrunning the second that he let his guard down.

On The Road Again

Pomona Freeway 6:20 PM

Mr. Pym was anxious to get back home.

Sure, it was an exciting trip on the way back, in fact, a bit TOO exciting. Right now he wanted nothing better than a relaxing shower and some sleep.

He liked Patrick and Danny.

Those guys were usually well behaved for boys. They took their initiations well.

He tried not to think about whatever it was that hit his car.

*

Danny wasn't quite sure what was bugging Patrick but he knew that something was freaking him out.

"Y'okay?"

"Sure Dan. I'm okay."

"Ya wanna come over and play Castlevania?"

"Maybe later."

It wasn't like Patrick to be so hesitant. He was usually a "yes or no" kind of kid. Danny liked "yes or no" kind of kids. He was straightforward and didn't take no bull from anybody. Patrick could be pretty cool when he wanted to be.

They also had fun when they "pal"ed around together.

That's the real reason Danny liked him. Patrick was fun.

His mom had that cool, gross out job working for the police.

That must be rad working with cops and catching crooks with high tech stuff like Robocop.

Danny's dad was an actuary. That was okay except when Dad would talk about people dying he never actually poked around in their bellies and stuff. That must be rad!

Traffic was slowing the Rambler down as they approached the city. In the distance, the tall library tower loomed above the rest of the buildings like a giant nail sticking out of a circuit board. A semi was pulled over on the shoulder of the road with a highway patrol car nuzzling behind it.
Its flashers winking a silent warning to the other drivers.

"I'll bet it's really something dumb, like the guy going over the old "double-nickel" as Gramps use to say," he thought.

Gramps was a trucker. He taught Danny all about the lingo of the open road.

When Danny was old enough to drive legally, he wanted to drive a truck cross-country with Grandpa, if possible.

Maybe he would invite Patrick.

Danny turned.

Patrick was starting to look better.

Suddenly, Patrick winced.

"What's happening, Tenderloin?"

"Ugh."

"Gonna barf?"

"Naw, I'm okay."

Danny followed Patrick's eyes out the window of the moving car. The light must have been playing tricks with his eyes. When he blinked the first time, Danny thought he saw something dark and huge running next to the freeway on the other side of the meridian.

He blinked again.

Whatever it was he was looking at was gone.

Protection

Feingold Residence
Los Angeles 6:20 PM

Jacqui Feingold looked at her olive skin in the reflective surface on the top of her stove and for a moment, thought she was on a beach somewhere just waking up by herself.

Nope, no such luck.

Her husband hadn't come home and said he just won the California State Lottery. The twins didn't stop hitting each other for five seconds while she was finishing dinner. Her entire family hadn't vanished painlessly leaving her all the imaginary lottery loot. All she wanted to do was watch an episode of "Love Connection" without having to worry about the steaks burning, Greg complaining that his balls itched after work or one of the twins coming home from school and asking her what a "beejay" was.

Darrin and Marvin Feingold were exchanging rabbit punches in what seemed to be an endless game of "I Got You Last" while Chuck Wollery listened to a mean-sounding stockbroker who was complaining that her date didn't spend enough money on her.

Merde, Jacqui thought. The way that bitch looked she was a fine one to talk.

She turned away from the TV in the living room and continued the seasoning of the T-bones. She bent over and readjusted the tray on the broiler.

"Stop hitting each other this instant, you guys, or I'll effing clobber you."

"Ohhhhh, Mommy said that naughty word, Darrin."

The other seven year old covered his mouth with his hand.

"Daddy's going to hit you, Mommy. We'll tell him to, huh, Marvin?"

"I'm going to tell him that the reason you aren't going to have any dinner tonight is because we used the steaks to cover your black eyes and swollen butts!"

That quieted the little monsters for a few seconds while they weighed their chances of mom bluffing or not.

Sheesh.

She hated to talk to the kids that way but they were getting too damn smart for the same psychological crap that her French parents used to use on her when she was growing up. Like Gregg, her husband said, "Sometimes parenting is just taking turns being the bad cop."

"Mommy, I got Darrin last. Ha ha ha ha."

"Did not", the twin pinched his brother's elbow.

The phone rang drowning out the yelp. She scooped it up on the first ring.

I hope it is Gregg and that he tells me that we've either won the lottery or that the children aren't really ours..

"Hello? Feingold zoo. Cage keeper Jacqui speaking."

"Jacqui? Hi. It's Jan. Did I catch you at a bad time?"

Jacqui turned briefly and looked at her boys.

The twins started wrestling.

"Stop that! No worse than usual. What's up?"

"Big favor. Could you pick up Patrick from my house when he comes back from his campout and feed him just for tonight? I'll return the favor for your kids next weekend if you like."

She looked at the little darlings. They had separated but were eyeing each other with evil eyes. School wasn't starting soon enough as far as Jacqui was concerned. She had a couple of extra T-bones. Patrick lived next door.

Heck, he was one of the few well-behaved kids who Jacqui actually liked. Gregg could take her to that snappy new Thai place next weekend and a movie while Jan watched the kids.

"No problem, honey. What time is he suppose to be home? I can run over next door and wait for him if you like with the little monsters. Gregg had some office work to do. We were going to cook outside but our grill is rusted to pieces."

"Not necessary for you to wait outside but thanks. You can call over there, if you want, since he's due any time now. He may want to shower or something first. I really appreciate this, Jacqui."

"As long as you know what you are setting yourself up for when it's your turn to watch my darlings."

She heard Jan chuckle on the other side of the line.

"The twins are fine. Thanks again and I'll be home to pick up Patrick as soon as things slow down here at work.

"Okay. See you." She replaced the phone on its cradle. The steaks were burning like little bovine Joan of Arcs.

Crap. Screw it. If worse comes to worse we'll go for burgers and soft-serve ice cream at Foster's.

Gregg, dear, you better have won the lottery...

*

The water spirit in the house heard something and moved towards to the front door.

"Hello? Patrick? Home yet? It's me, Jacqui."

The water spirit tried to reach a watery tendril from under the door.

Too late.

The woman was gone.

*

Jacqui didn't hear anything and figured that he wasn't home yet. She returned home unaware of the long, thin blue cord of liquid that narrowly missed looping itself around her ankles.

*

Across town Jan and Ron were having a conversation with a scruffy Latino man wearing a light green shirt and white pants. Felipe Munoz was in his thirties and had about six tattoos displayed between his fingers on his right arm. He was once in a gang and the markings on his fingers showed him as a "bird dog" or "scout" for suckers. He would look for people he could scam or run cons on.

Jan wasn't going to complain. Most of the crimes solved with gangs involved the use of informants such as this mean, nervous punk.

The place they met him at smelled of French fries. They had arrived quietly without fanfare at a small, Mexican burger joint just a few blocks away from headquarters at the man's request. He had responded to a television plea for information and he didn't want to meet the police at the station.

He sent his fellow homeboys away earlier so nobody would know that he was dealing with the law.

Jan thought this guy was a real beaut. From what his rap sheet said, he had a long history of juvenile crimes before graduating into extortion, con games, smuggling and whatever else he could turn a buck with. His known associates numbered in the dozens. Even though he no longer kept company with known street gangs, he knew what was going on in the streets.

They sat at a small, wooden table. Felipe began twirling the saltshaker around nervously with his fingers.

"Hi, Felipe. Something bugging you?"

Ron was leaning across from him practically in his face.

"Yeah, your ugly nose. Move it back."

Ron leaned back in his chair. He turned towards Jan.

"Felipe and I are old friends."

"I am gonna blow this town and I wanna get high."

Jan introduced herself. She continued speaking softly. "I can't help you get high but can I get you something to drink?"

He smiled and displayed his lemon yellow teeth and blackened fillings. "Since I can't have a doobie, Coke, por favor."

Ron stood up. He walked casually to the counter. They were the only people in the place. It was the evening of a Labor Day holiday. Those people who weren't barbecuing their dinners at home on their grills were throwing theirs up from drinking too much.

Jan stared at Felipe. She hoped Patrick would never turn out like this. Felipe was in his twenties but he looked like he was in his forties. He continued twirling the salt shaker.

Ron returned with the soda and Munoz took like a chimpanzee stealing peanuts at the zoo. Discreetly, Ron dropped a crumpled one hundred dollar bill on the table in front of Munoz. With his free hand,

Felipe Munoz scooped the bill up. He quickly deposited his snitch money inside his pants pocket.

"This all you got? Where's the big money?"

"If it leads to an arrest, you'll get ten thousand dollars later."

"Screw later. For now, man, you gotta send somebody to protect me please."

Ron returned to his seat. He took a long, luxurious breath before continuing. "Give us something that will lead to an arrest, Munoz. What can you tell us about these killings."

Felipe Munoz drank some of his Coke. He replaced the half-empty glass on the counter with a dull thud.

"The loco who is doing all this is Jorge Longrunning. This dude calls me up out of the blue a few days ago. He says he is going to whack me, tu savvy?" Munoz

paused, took another long pull on his soda.
"Man, this joker said he was going to get me
and ruin me, y'know? I tell him, name the
time and I'll name the place and let's do
this right away because I don't take crap
from anybody! So I went to Stella's, one of
those pay for dance halls for wets."

"Wets? As in wetbacks? Aren't you
from Mexico, Munoz?" Ron asked.

"Ha but I am citified. This place caters
to Peruvians as well as Mexicans and all
sorts of South American homeboys who
want some company, some familiarity,
some songs and mostly to score with a
woman." He looked at Jan for a reaction.

Seeing none, his gaze returned to Ron.

"How much of that are you into,
Felipe?"

Munoz's eyes darted around the room.

"I don't follow you, man."

Ron leaned forward again.

"So you had your homies waiting for him and something went south, huh?"

The young man's face went white. "Man, it was something out of a George Romero movie. I was waiting outside and all of a sudden I heard these screams. I figure something really nasty was going down. I raced inside and found three of my soldiers beheaded. Their bodies were pulped and their heads were placed on plates next to beer mugs full of their own blood. The placed smelled like an embalming room."

"How come they didn't make it to the morgue?"

"We take care of our own here. It's like that. I had a funeral home dude I know clean up the mess and ditch the heads. I paid off the people at Stella's to keep it quiet. Then, get this; I get a phone call from Jorge saying that he's busy and sorry he missed me. Listen, all my business has dried up and most of my men are staying away from me as if I had smallpox. I'm thinkin' this is a good time to go straight but I don't want this guy hounding my butt. I need some help."

"Did he say why he wanted to kill you?" Ron asked.

"He mumbled some crap about his son. Told me some name. Don't remember it."

"What name?"

"His son's name. Some name. I don't remember it, okay? At this point, I don't want to remember. All I can get from the word on the street is that this guy runs a cleaning supplies business. Nobody can find him unless he wants to be found, y'know? I can tell you this: I tried hiding out at three different places and he telephoned me each time just to say 'hi'. I'm totally loco now and I need your protection."

"Munoz, without any bodies, all we have is your story that you are being threatened. That isn't a basis for getting protection."

"Haven't you been listening to anything I've said? Go to Stella's and tell them it was cool to talk to you. Please."

"They are on your payroll. Not reliable. Produce the bodies of your dead homies."

"Argggh. They were cremated, man."

Ron stood up. "Well, no bodies, no protection. That's that. Come on, doctor."

Jan stood up. "Thank you for your time and good luck."

They left the restaurant under a blistering tirade of Mexican curses.

Outside Jan moved closer to Ron. She continued to look straight ahead and ignore the two plainclothes cops that had moved in. They were watching the restaurant from across the street.

One was a Latino man wearing a jacket and reading a copy of "LA OPINION". The other was an allegedly elderly man picking his nose. He was drinking from a bottle in a sack.

"We've got a name at last. Jorge Longrunning. If this clown comes near Felipe Munoz, our guys will call in back up and grab him. We've two units circling the neighborhood who are ordered to respond to them as their number one priority."

Jan and Ron stopped at a crosswalk.

The light flashed red.

"I wasn't too comfortable terrorizing him like that," Jan stated.

"When you consider all the people he's terrorized or try to con over the years, I think we still went easy on him. Better for him to think he isn't being protected to draw out Jorge Longrunning."

Ron was right. At least they had some more leads to add to the case. Jorge Longrunning had a son.

Was that what she picked up on earlier?

His son.

Her son.

Jan felt a cold, tingling racing up and down her spine like somebody was dancing on her grave. She looked around and thought she caught a glimpse of something glowing from behind an alley. Something that was staring at her. She blinked and it was gone.

*

Jorge Longrunning ducked into a manhole. He had an appointment he had to keep.

Overtime

Jan's Lab 7:05 PM

Everybody but Myra had left the lab. Some people were taking a break for dinner and were going to return. Others had knocked off for the day.

Myra was by herself.

She was sorting manila folders when she saw the bucket.

Those stupid cleaning people.

She tried calling Vince one more time. He never got back in touch with her. His line was busy.

To heck with Vince.

She rubbed her eyes and arched her back like a cat.

She walked over to the bucket.

The Visit

Jan's Office 7:10 PM

Ron had left Jan's office briefly to see if anything could be found on Jorge Longrunning. Jan was in her office cleaning the top of her desk and rechecking some lab results.

She saw something.

The glass windows to the corridor started fogging up.

Like something out of the tropics.

It was the same feeling she had when she was talking to Injun Joe.

She looked out the window into the hallway.

A tall man was wringing a mop into a bucket.

She raced into the hallway.

The man was leisurely mopping the floor in complete sidestrokes.   He was very precise and thorough.

"I'm almost done cleaning."

He looked familiar.

"Jorge Longrunning? I know you from somewhere before."

"Yes, we met."

He placed the mop down and pulled out his half of the book, Lowerworld.

Jan reached into her pocket and pulled out the pages she had.

She was whooshed into the book.

*

Inside the book, she saw Jorge Longrunning. It looked like she was still standing in the hallway except when she looked down, she didn't have the book pages in her hand and neither did Jorge.

"I came here to claim my son Peter's body. I never got a chance to show you what happened did I?"

He raised his hand and the air shimmered around her. Pictures and movies materialized like she was at the Imax Theater.

*

Peter Longrunning was sipping from his soda bottle in the small restaurant in Baja, California. The eighteen year-old from Ecuador had about $250 left to his name from all of the odd jobs he had taken to make it this close to the United States. He hoped it would be enough.

Despite his father's warnings of possible bad tidings, Peter wanted to see the land from where all those movies came from.

From the American movies, everything looked so big and clean in America!

Rico Estavez entered the restaurant and waved at Peter.

Peter returned the wave and motioned him to his table.

"We're almost ready," Rico stated in Spanish, "Let's go".

Peter nervously got out of his chair. He downed the rest of his soda. Tiny droplets of sweet cola remained on his lips.

Rico put his arm around Peter. He escorted him out of the cantina.

It was good to be outside again.

Such good fortune to find a friend like Rico who will help me get to the United States, too.

"Have the money?" Estavez asked.

"It's right here," Peter pulled the two hundred and fifty dollars in twenties and a single ten out of his pocket. Rico plucked the money out of his fingers like a bird yanking a worm out of the ground.

"For this kind of money, the best thing I can do is get you the economy trip, tu savy? It goes like this: we will hide you in the back of a car's trunk and we will drive across into the United States. When we get to the other side, we let you out and we have a job waiting for you."

A job in America! In California!

Maybe it would be for one of those big, wonderful movie studios.

"I trust you, Rico. You are very honest."

The coyote smiled. "Let's go".

They walked for several blocks and turned into an alley.

Peter had worked two years and had made it all the way up from his home in Ecuador. He had made it to Tijuana from Ensenada after working on a boat that came up the western coast of Baja California from South America.

He was so close to his destination that he could almost see all of the movie stars walking down the Hollywood streets waving and smiling at tourists.

In the alley was a large, brown car. It looked like it was ready to fall apart. On one side of the car were five other young men who looked as anxious as Peter. On the right side were the Delgado brothers and Felipe Gomez.

Gomez had opened the trunk and it was huge.

Like a giant bear's jaws.

"Bueno. Everybody is here," Rico motioned Peter towards the trunk. "You get in first, Peter. The trip is very short and there will be a good hearty meal, clean clothes and your job waiting for you on the other side."

This is so wonderful.

The other five men climbed in on top of him blocking out the sun. The metal of the trunk was hot and the thick serape that was lined on the bottom of the trunk seemed to make it more stifling.

Ugh. They were heavy.

It was uncomfortable for Peter Longrunning.

The lid closed and he could hear the laughing of the Delgado brothers and slamming of car doors as they got into the car. The other men in the trunk with him were starting to cough as the car's engine turned over.

The exhaust system of the car was tied directly into the trunk. The pipe was spewing carbon monoxide into the young men's faces.

Peter was not aware of this. He thought it was a slight passing discomfort at first. He and the other men started coughing, gagging and dry retching as the car drove through the streets of Tijuana and finally came to a rest in an abandoned lot filled with the shells of older cars. Several fires burned nearby.

The mobile gas chamber was cranked up and Peter Longrunning and the others died an uncomfortable, suffocating death two hours after the coyotes had placed them in it.

They opened the trunk, took the bodies and sold them to a man who shipped them to Los Angeles for use as practice cadavers.

Their bodies were filled with formaldehyde.

*

Jan blinked. She was still in the book but understood what was going on.

"I remember when the police brought me their bodies. You had come up and claimed his body. You identified him."

"Yes. I was taking him back home when I was in a large car accident and I was killed. At the moment I was killed part of the book that you have the other part of came in contact with me and I was able to bring myself back."

"What does this have to do with me?"

"I want your pages from the book so I can bring back my son from the dead. If you don't give them to me, I will kill your son and your assistant."

Jorge Longrunning raised his hand and two blue water spirits appeared and flowed towards Jan.

Instinctively, she raised her hands to her face and screamed, "No.".

The water spirits splashed on her arms and receded to the ground.

"It's the pages of the book that I have," she said. "They must be protecting me."

"You don't have the will power to stop me."

Two men in togas appeared before them.

"You have to rejoin the pages of the book."

"Who are you two?" Jan asked.

"We're the spirits of the book, Lowerworld. One of us is from the half of the book that you have, Jan, and the other is from the half that Jorge Longrunning has."

"Give me the pages, Jan Brighton, or your son and your friend will die."

"No".

"Very well, watch."

The blue water spirits on the floor shot up like a fountain. Inside the fountain, Jan could see Myra trying to scream. In a second, Myra stopped moving.

Her body slumped to the ground.

She reached over. Myra was dead.

"You bastard."

"Your son is next. If you don't give me the half of the book you have."

"Don't do it," said one of the people in the toga. "Fight him."

"Give him the pages", the other person in the toga said. "You are weak."

The spirits here are as split as the book pages, Jan thought.

Jan was filled with rage.

"Don't threaten me or my son." She raced towards Jorge Longrunning.

She hit the wall of the hallway.

She was back in the real world.

Slumped on the ground next to her was the dead body of Myra.

Racing Home

Jan's Lab 7:20 PM

Jan was racing down the hall to Ron's office. Ron was scanning the papers from the fax machine when Jan burst in on him and the clerk who worked the desk.

"Ron, he was here and he killed Myra."

"Who?"

"Jorge Longrunning. The janitor. You won't believe what is going on but I need you to come with me and we've got to get to Patrick."

"Myra is dead?"

"Yes, call some patrol cars to go watch my house and for goodness sake we've got to hurry!"

Rest In Peace Felipe Gomez

Felipe Gomez's apartment   7:26 PM

The bear spirit had crashed into the apartment building that Felipe Gomez was hiding in.

Felipe Gomez was watching the news. If Felipe thought things were bleak for Los Angeles, they were about to get downright dismal for him. Before he could even turn his head completely around or reach for the pump shotgun that was sitting on his lap, the bear took a swipe at his head and separated it completely from his body.

Blood fountained out of the gaping neck while the weatherman forecasted an unusually cloudy night and possible showers.

One of Felipe's guards had opened the door and pointed his shotgun at the bear.

He pulled the trigger.

The bear ran into the blast, absorbed the impact of the hot stream of lead shot. He took a bite into the man's face.

He started gnawing at the rest of the struggling hood's body.

When the bear would get a chance he would do the same thing to Jorge Longrunning.

Finally Home

Jan and Patrick's House 7:28 PM

"Okay, Patrick. See ya."

"Bye, Mr. Pym. Later, Danny."

"Good-bye."

They had finished unloading the gear that belonged to Patrick along the curb and Patrick waved his farewell to Mr. Pym and Danny. The Rambler drove off.

It was good to be home. It was nice that Jacqui was outside waiting for him and nicer that Mom had called in advance to see if he was okay.

At that point, the water spirit smashed open the front door and lunged towards Patrick.

Patrick screamed and everything was covered with sand. Jacqui was getting up from the street muttering to herself.

The entire street was covered with sand. The water spirit was covered with sand and started falling to the ground in clumped, moist sand globs.

Patrick blinked.

Standing next to him was the boy Leo and next to him was the little dog, Woofy. They were from the book that was scrunched in his pocket.

"We've got to find your mother, kid." Leo said.

"What's going on?"

"The short form of the story kid is that I was escorting a very powerful book back to the ancient Library of Alexandria when we got into a car accident. A crazy dead guy who wanted revenge so badly came back from the dead when the book we were sent to bring back, the Lowerworld was torn in half. One half is in the hands of this crazy dead guy and the other is in your Mom's hands. Did I miss anything, Woofy?"

Woofy shook his head sideways indicating "no".

"Good. Kid, wish all the sand away."

"Huh?"

"Are you deaf? I said wish for all the sand to go away."

"Uh, okay, I wish the sand would go away."

The sand was gone.

"Okay, excuse yourself from that lady and let's find your mom."

"Huh?"

"Now, kid. Now!"

A Couple Blocks Away

Jan and Ron were driving the van and came to a complete stop when she saw Patrick running in the street towards her. Next to him were a boy and a dog.

The two police cars that were escorting her pulled over as well.

Jan jumped out of the car.

"Patrick, are you okay?"

"Mom! I missed you!"

They ran and collided in a locking hug. The policemen and Ron approached the other boy.

"Who are you, son?" Ron asked.

"My actual name is Leonidas Oyzmandias but you may call me Leo. Also, I am not your son."

"Woof," said Woofy.

A giant stream of blue water erupted next to the people from a sewer entrance. The sewer cap slammed into the roof of one of the police cars. The stream of water formed into a giant hand and smashed into the other police car.

Jorge Longrunning was standing on top of a fountain of water. The water gently lowered him back to the ground.

"Give me your half of the book," he commanded to Jan.

"No, you give your half of the book to her," Leo countered.

"Grrrrrr", growled Woofy.

A giant roar came up from the sewer. The street cracked as a giant brown bear lumbered to the surface. It was twenty feet tall.

It approached Jorge Longrunning. Jorge pulled his half of the book out of his pocket.

"I command you to kill them."

The bear leaned forward and bit off Jorge Longrunning's head.

"I've had enough of you and I was going to do that anyways."

Jorge's lifeless body fell to the ground fountaining blood. He released his grip on his half of the book.

Jan dove forward and grabbed it. She lifted her copy of the book and electrical energy crackled between the pages. In a matter of seconds the books was whole again.

"How come the water monster and bear are still here?"

The water monster smashed the police cars. The officers were trying to empty their guns into the water monster and bear.

The bear lunged at a policeman. It wasn't pretty.

"We have to destroy these spirits. They don't want to get back into the book. They don't want to be part of the Library anymore, kid." Leo said.

"How? How are we going to do that?"

"Think of sand, the desert, any of that stuff and leave the rest to me. Your thoughts and wishing are what gives me strength."

Patrick started thinking about the pyramids of Egypt, of the Sphinx.

"Good ones!"

Leo screamed and tore off his face. Underneath, he had sand formed features that started growing. In seconds he was larger than the water spirit and looked like he was a walking pyramid.

Jan looked up and realized they were in harms way. She motioned for Patrick, Ron and the remaining policemen to run away from the titans.

Woofy roared and grew into a giant sphinx. Woofy grabbed the bear with his front paws and started chewing into his neck.

Leo literally sat down on the water spirit smashing the pavement and causing car alarms to go off all along the street.

Jan tried to cover Patrick but they were thrown apart. Ron bounced on top of a car as the buildings on the street started to buckle.

"Mom!" Patrick screamed.

"I'm okay! How are you?" she yelled back.

"Fine!" He screamed.

With a flash of light and electricity, the bear and water spirits were gone. Leo and Woofy started shrinking and turned back to normal.

"Great job, kid."

"Uh, thanks."

"Now get the book from your Mom and I want you to call a guy named Mr. Ptolemy in New Alexandria California and tell him to send down a car for us."

Woofy started barking rhythmically.

"Woofy is going to make people forget all of this happened- with the exception of you and your Mom. If you ever move to New Alexandria, California, look us up."

Leo and Woofy faded away.

He pulled the book out of the back of his pants pocket.

The book looked the same.

Except for the wreckage on the street and the dead bodies, everything was okay.

Jan looked at the book and the street.

She shrugged her shoulders and hugged her son.

Patrick was delighted, excited and at the same time relieved. He didn't think he would want to move to New Alexandria anytime soon.

The Good Life

September 4, 1990
Jan's House 12:00 PM

Jan and Ron were washing their car down in front of their new house. They were married after they had found the corpse of the man they later named "The Clean Killer". How he managed to also kill all the policemen before dying was a mystery to everybody. The good thing was that he was dead.

Patrick banged open the front door. He raced outside.

"Danny just called me. Mom, one more campout before school starts?"

"If it's okay with your father, sure." She glanced at Ron.

"Sure, Patrick, just remember to go easy on the Tenderfeet, okay?"

He rolled his eyes. "I remember, Dad. I know how much I hated it when I was a Tenderfoot."

Ron smiled.

Jan smiled and reached for the window cleaner.

She looked closely at the spray bottle.

She thought she saw some bubbling inside.

Maybe it was time that they seriously thought about moving to New Alexandria, California...

THE   END

www.ingramcontent.com/pod-product-compliance
Lightning Source LLC
Chambersburg PA
CBHW031216020726
47499CB00002B/608